I0531075

THE NORTHLAND CHRONICLES:
SPEAR HUNTER

HENRY J. OLSEN

Copyright © 2015 by Henry J. Olsen

I encourage you to share this book with others. You may even make copies for private use. Though reading is often a solitary experience, good books are meant to be copied, passed around, and enjoyed.

Selling unauthorized copies for profit is a different matter. Should you try to profit from my work without my express permission, you may soon hear an angry knock on your door from a certain bionic-armed gunslinger ...

ISBN: 978-0-9894193-6-9

Unbound Adventure Press
P.O. Box 27
Black Earth, WI 53515

http://simplyunbound.com

Cover photo by Randen Petersen. Used in accordance with the terms of the CC BY 2.0 license.

For my mother
The most vocal supporter
a son could hope for

I'd like to thank the following people for helping to make *Spear Hunter* a thrilling island adventure.

Brendan Beltz
Charles Borchert
Chris Garland
John Maresco
Gary Olsen
Gaila Olsen
Stephen Robak

"When you saved us back there ... you knew you were firing a slug, not buckshot, right?"
"I'm going to pretend you didn't ask me that."

Prologue

IT HAD TAKEN nearly nine years, but finally the world was putting itself back together.

Captain Griswold sat at a circular table inside the Snowdrift Cafe, nervously tapping his feet to the beat of the vintage folk music playing on the stereo. He sipped his imitation coffee, relishing the rich scent as he watched the light drizzle outside.

Coffee, shelter, and music — what more could a man ask for? Despite the vast swaths of buildings that remained uninhabited and desolate, Toronto was beginning to feel like a real city once again.

Griswold glanced at his wind-up watch. Officer Leon was late. Griswold scratched at the shriveled scar tissue where his right ear had once been. Only at nerve-racking times like these did he remember the ear was gone.

Was Officer Leon rejecting his request for a meeting? She hadn't left the Toronto police force on amicable terms and was in no way obliged to meet him, but Griswold believed that she would come. Curiosity would compel her to hear him out, if not agree to his suggestion.

Raindrops pattered against the panes of the coffee shop's large storefront windows. Beyond the glass, Griswold saw a bright crimson figure trudging through the gloomy mist outside. Officer Leon, perhaps? Before he could be certain, a tvapa-drawn wagon pulled in front of the window, obscuring his view.

The coffee shop's barista, a young, dark woman with deep, soulful eyes, came over to wipe down the adjacent table. She smiled at Griswold as she scrubbed the circular slab of varnished hardwood.

"Is it always this quiet on weekends?" Griswold asked her. Besides the barista and himself, the only other souls in the cafe were an elderly man and woman seated in the back corner.

The barista shook her head. "Nah, today is slow for a Saturday. I think the rain is keeping people away. Not that I can complain — I appreciate a slow day every once in a while. How is the chicory root brew treating you?"

"I'm enjoying it," Griswold remarked. "Honestly, it's been so long since I've had real coffee that I can hardly remember what the genuine article tastes like."

"You and everyone else in North America, I imagine." The barista beamed at him. "If you hear of anyone who's figured out how to grow coffee beans in Canada, let us know."

"You'll be the first one I call," Griswold said with a wink. "Once I find the coffee and a working phone."

The barista chuckled. "Sounds like I might be waiting a while."

The cafe's door chime jingled, drawing Griswold's attention to the entrance. He raised his hand to greet the newcomer, Officer Leon.

"Looks like your company has arrived." The barista lifted her wiping cloth from the table and drifted away.

Officer Leon lowered the hood of her sweatshirt as she approached Griswold's table. Droplets of water trickled down from her red sleeves onto the hardwood floor.

"A crimson hoodie? I never knew you to wear such garish colors, Officer Leon."

"Says the man in a purple Toronto Raptors t-shirt," Officer Leon shot back.

Griswold looked down at his t-shirt. "Fair enough. Have a seat, will you?"

Officer Leon eyed Griswold warily, then sat down across from him. Not even her impatient expression could hide the natural beauty of her thin lips, soft nose, and smooth skin. In addition to the red sweatshirt, she wore blue jeans and had a revolver holstered on her hip. The revolver was the largest Griswold had ever seen, a make he didn't recognize.

Officer Leon crossed her arms. "So, why'd you call me here, Griswold?"

"Well, you see, Officer Le —"

"I turned in my badge," Officer Leon cut in. "That means I'm not an officer anymore."

"Alright, then what should I —"

"And I hope you're not here to try to lure me back into the Toronto PD, because I highly doubt anything has changed in the past few months since I left."

Griswold sighed. "Do we have to have this conversation again? Look, I know you have misgivings about the way I run the police department."

"Well, forgive me if I have 'misgivings' about how your department keeps cold-blooded killers on the payroll," Officer Leon said with a scowl.

"We've been over this before. Police morale is already in the dumps, and I can't afford to decommission officers every time one of them has a lapse in judgme —"

"A lapse in judgment?" Officer Leon snapped, rising from her chair. "You and I both know that what I saw was hardly a 'lapse in judgment'."

"Hear me out, Officer," Griswold pleaded.

Officer Leon shook her head. "Why did I even bother coming here?" she grumbled, making her way for the exit.

Griswold frowned, pursing his lips. He understood why she loathed the Toronto PD, but this wasn't about his police force, or even about Toronto. *If only she'd listen, she would see that*, he thought.

"Tell me, officer — why did you join my force in the first place?" Griswold called out across the room.

Officer Leon stopped in her tracks, pausing to consider the question. The folk song playing in the background faded out, and the intro to another tune followed shortly, an impassioned mix of lethargic rhythm guitar and wailing blues harmonica.

"Because I wanted to help people. I wanted to give them hope in the Desolation's wake," she said, her back still facing Griswold.

"That's a noble end. How have you been working toward it in the months since you left?" Griswold asked. When Officer

Leon offered no reply, he continued, "I know there is corruption in my force, and I know you're not comfortable with that. That's why I asked you here today as a personal favor. It's why I'm wearing this ugly t-shirt instead of my uniform. Because while my force has issues — major issues — I, William Ebeneezer Griswold, personally want to make this world a better place. And I need your help."

Officer Leon crossed her arms. She tapped her finger against her elbow, thoughtfully. The strumming of a lone acoustic guitar reverberated from the cafe's stereo.

"I know it's not my place, but I think you should hear the man out," a gravelly male voice said. "He seems like a decent fellow."

Griswold looked over his shoulder. The words came from the elderly man who'd been sitting in the corner, now heading toward the exit with his female companion.

"But don't mind me. I'm sure I don't know the half of it," he added, smiling as he walked past Officer Leon. "Come on, dear," he said, holding the door open for his companion before following her into the dreary afternoon rain.

Griswold watched through the window as the man opened an umbrella and held it above his companion's head. The couple sauntered away, soon walking beyond the edge of the glass windowpane and disappearing from sight.

Officer Leon stepped back to Griswold's table. She reclaimed her seat and gave him a cold, hard stare.

"Alright, William Ebeneezer Griswold, let's hear what it is you have to say," she said. Her expression had softened, and Griswold now saw traces of the ambitious youngster he'd once eagerly welcomed into his force.

"Have you heard of the General?" he asked.

"The General?" Officer Leon repeated, her thin lips forming a hint of a smirk. "No, but I have heard of the Queen of Spain, the Prime Minister, and Santa Claus."

"I'm being serious, Officer —"

"Call me Aristotle."

"Aristotle?" Griswold grimaced, scratching at his stub of a right ear.

"It's a nickname I picked up while I was drifting around up north." She pulled back the right sleeve of her crimson sweatshirt, revealing a tattoo inked across her wrist. Griswold didn't recognize the script. Presumably, it was Greek for "Aristotle."

"Look, if you don't want me to call you 'Officer,' why don't I just call you by your real name?"

"Because I've begun a new chapter," she said. "And a new chapter calls for a new name."

Griswold shook his head, exasperated. "Suit yourself, Aristotle."

"Anyway, continue."

"Right — the General. Over the last few months our radio room has been picking up bits and pieces of stray radio chatter. It caught us by surprise, quite frankly, as radios aren't exactly a hot item these days."

"I know I haven't seen any, outside the few that your department has."

"Exactly. At first we weren't sure what to make of the chatter, but quickly it became clear that the transmissions were between members of some sort of army or militia, led by a man who calls himself the General. Just as we were putting the pieces together, however, the transmissions suddenly stopped."

"Just stopped?" Aristotle raised an eyebrow.

"A few weeks ago. We've heard nothing but static since then. We suspect that someone found out we were listening and decided to jam the frequency, but my department has neither the expertise nor the resources to look into what happened."

"Isn't investigating leads like this part of your job, *Captain* Griswold?"

Griswold frowned. "It's not that simple. You see, the transmissions originated from far outside our jurisdiction."

"Oh?" Aristotle's face lit up.

"We couldn't pinpoint exactly where the signals were coming from, but most of the conversations included locational information — the speakers referring to lakes and other landmarks. After poring over a number of maps, we ascertained that most of the transmissions were coming from northern Minnesota."

"Radios can broadcast that far?"

"If atmospheric conditions are perfect, perhaps, but even accounting for that the range is quite impressive. We haven't been able to determine how they're broadcasting their signals over such a wide area. In any case, I'm less concerned about the technical details of the radio transmissions and more concerned about their content, which brings us back to the General. It seems he's building an army, recruiting disillusioned young men for an armed takeover of Minnesota and perhaps beyond."

Aristotle tapped her fingers on the table. "Any idea why he's setting up operations in Minnesota?"

Griswold shrugged. "Your guess is as good as mine."

"And what makes you think he hopes to expand his influence beyond Minnesota?"

"In my experience, power hungry men don't let borders stop them, especially when they're looking at hazy, unprotected borders like the ones established by the fledgling Republic of Minnesota."

Aristotle leaned back in her chair and crossed her arms. "So, what do you want me to do?"

"Recon. I want you to go to Minnesota and see what you can find out about the General. I've compiled a list of the landmarks mentioned by the radio operators. It'll be a good starting point at least." Griswold pulled a piece of paper from the pocket of his khakis and offered it to Aristotle. When she made no move to accept it, he set it on the table.

"And that's all you have to go on?" she asked.

"Yeah, I'm afraid that's about it."

Aristotle furrowed her brow. "You honestly expect me to just drop everything and go stomping around Minnesota to chase after this guy, based on a few meager scraps of evidence you've scrounged together?"

"Well, when you put it that way —"

She stood up from her chair. "I think it's awfully presumptuous of you to assume that I have nothing better to do with my time than take care of the menial tasks that you and your cesspool of a police department don't want to bother yourselves with."

"Hey now, I thought we were done talking about my —"

"You know, Griswold," she said, snatching the piece of paper from the table. "I think you're a decent man, but you really should get a handle on your own affairs here in Toronto before you start shoving your nose into Minnesota business." She slid the paper into her back pocket and began to walk away.

Griswold's mouth jaw hung open. Was she accepting his request? As she neared the door, she paused for a moment.

"Say, Griswold." She turned to look at him.

"Yes?"

"You ever hear of a man, goes by the name of John Osborne? Bit of a loner, knows how to fight."

"Can't say that I have," Griswold cocked his head. "Why?"

"No reason. Just curious."

"Okay ..." Griswold trailed off. He'd never heard of this man, John Osborne.

"We'll be in touch, Griswold." The door chimes clanged together as Aristotle pushed the front door open and walked out into the gray afternoon. She threw up her hood and proceeded down the street, seemingly oblivious to the raindrops seeping into the fabric of her sweatshirt.

"She's got zeal. I'll give her that."

Griswold jerked in his chair, instinctively reaching to cover his right ear. He'd forgotten that he and Aristotle hadn't been alone.

"That's what I like about her," he said, craning his neck toward the front counter where the barista was standing, polishing a coffee mug. "She's got an inner compass that always leads her in the right direction, a compass truer than I could ever hope to have."

"I'm sure you have a hard job, Captain. Give yourself a little credit." She smiled at him, then turned and disappeared into a back room behind the counter.

Griswold returned to his chicory root coffee, now lukewarm. He sat quietly, wondering if it'd been wise to enlist Aristotle's help and send her into the unknown. As he pondered the decision, folk music continued to play in the background.

A hard rain was gonna fall.

Chapter 1

JOHN STARED INTO the orange glow of his modest campfire, watching the fire consume the dry birch, pine, and ash he'd fed it. Twisting scarves of smoke rose from the burning wood, listlessly rising through the windless evening air.

As John sat motionlessly on his log, he heard a dull buzz in his left ear. A quick swat of his hand silenced the noise. *Mosquitoes prefer stationary targets,* he thought. Perhaps the flying bloodsucker was letting him know that he'd overstayed his welcome. He'd been in Frontier View for nearly two weeks, already longer than he'd remained in any other place since his drift across the continent had begun nearly two years prior. Time to move along.

John started at the sound of a snapping twig, coming from just outside the level, grassy glade in which he'd pitched his tent. His right hand sprang to his revolver, a Colt Single Action Army. Drawing a deep, silent breath, he rubbed his thumb on the cool metal of the gun's hammer.

"That you, kid?" he called out into the darkness.

"Were you hoping for someone else?"

John relaxed, removing his hand from the holstered gun and resting his palms on his log.

"Your stealth needs work," John said.

"Who said I was trying to sneak up on you?" Nathan said as he perched beside John on the log, facing the fire.

John studied the kid, watching the shadows cast by the fire sweep across the hills and valleys of his face. He offered no reply.

The two men sat silently, hypnotized by the seductive glow. The campfire hissed as water trapped within a burning log broke free and evaporated into the balmy night air.

"How is your arm?" Nathan asked, leaning forward and resting his chin on his hands.

"Good as new," John replied, rubbing the scar tissue on his all-natural arm, his right. Just today, Cynthia had finally removed the bandages from the gunshot wound he'd sustained while rescuing Nathan's sister, Emiko, from kidnappers. John clenched his fist, noting the tightness in his wrist and forearm. Disuse had weakened his muscles, but soon his strength would return in full. It always did.

"And your other arm?" Nathan asked.

"No change. Functioning normally as far as I can tell, but I haven't had to tap its extra strength since Sawbill Lake."

"That's an improvement, I guess, isn't it?" Nathan offered. "Say, speaking of Sawbill Lake, do you think the info Ramses gave us is really gonna help? What do you think we're gonna find on Mallard Island?"

"Can't say, but it's the only lead we have."

"You're not worried that it could be a trap?"

John rubbed his beard. "If his sole intention was to set a trap, then he wouldn't have bothered sending us to such a remote location. That's not to say there won't be any danger, but I'm sure whoever told Ramses to send me to Mallard Island did so because of the piece of hardware grafted to my shoulder, and that means we might be able to learn more about it."

"But they could be telling you to go to Mallard Island for a reason unrelated to your arm."

John shook his head. "I doubt it. Aside from my left arm, I'm just another gun."

"But what if —"

"Give the questions a rest." John fixed his eyes on the fire. "We'll have plenty of time to talk on the road."

With a sigh, Nathan rose and walked to the stack of firewood John had gathered, picking up a stick of ash and offering it to the eager flames.

Is he up for this? John wondered. Despite his inclination to work alone, John had decided to take Nathan along. He'd agreed to do so because their first experience together had gone well, and also because Pierre had recommended it. Then again, Pierre wasn't exactly shy about making suggestions.

Nathan rearranged the embers with a long stick, causing sparks and smoke to mushroom up. After prodding the campfire he reclaimed his seat.

"Packed your bags?" John asked.

"Yeah. I'm ready to set out," Nathan said.

"Got our frankenmoose and cart ready?"

"You bet."

"Got plenty of ammo for your Remington?"

"Slugs and shot shells."

"Good. Then I'll see you bright and early tomorrow morning." John rose to his feet.

"Where are you going?" asked Nathan, suspiciously.

"There's someone I should say goodbye to. I won't be back for a few hours. Make sure the fire is under control before you leave."

"Got it," Nathan replied.

"Thanks, kid. Sleep well."

John's stomach growled as he stood. He'd been eating well in Frontier View — Cynthia had made sure of it — but no matter how much he ate there always seemed to be room for more. With a smack of his lips, he stepped into the tree cover that stood between his secluded tent site and Frontier View. As he made his way toward the village, he rubbed his left arm.

The arm felt like his. Even the hair felt real, the short, dark strands moving naturally as he swept his fingers across them. Despite its familiarity, however, John knew the arm had been given to him for reasons he didn't understand, much less trust.

Did the arm's capabilities come at a cost? What price was he paying each time he invoked its strength? Until John could answer those questions he would both respect and fear the arm, like a partner with motives unknown.

John left the woods and made his way through Frontier View. Two parallel rows of cabins, facing each other, formed the entirety of the small village. Though most of the cabin windows were dark, lamplight still lingered within a few of the homes. John stopped in front of one particular cabin and slowly pushed open the door. Despite the unlit interior, he was sure that the woman inside was still awake and waiting for him.

* * *

Nathan watched the dying campfire. When only glowing embers remained, he took his stick and separated the coals. Confident the fire wouldn't restart, Nathan started back toward his cabin, eager for sleep. Morning would come early.

Was he ready to leave Frontier View again? On the eve of his departure he was both excited and apprehensive. He looked forward to the new adventure, but feared leaving the safety of the village he called home. Memories of the last time he'd embarked on a long journey, a quest to save his father from illness, still weighed heavily on his heart. That trip had ended in crushing despair. Would this one fare better?

Fortunately, the circumstances of this new adventure were altogether different from his last. Nathan's father had been seeking medical help; John was merely looking for answers.

Despite his unease, Nathan was looking forward to accompanying John. Still, many questions remained. Could he earn John's trust? Would he be up to facing the trials of the road? Could he make himself useful, or would John come to see him as a burden? Nathan knew he could answer these questions by deed alone and was determined to prove himself worthy no matter what trials they encountered. He hoped to forge a closer bond with John and discover first-hand what gave the man his confidence and swagger.

Soon Nathan arrived at his cabin, opening the door carefully so as not to disturb Emiko. As he slipped into the bedroom he glanced at her. She lay atop the sheets of her bed, snoring gently. *I really hope she doesn't make a fuss tomorrow*, Nathan thought. His sister had yet to accept John's refusal to let her to join the expedition to Mallard Island.

Nathan yawned as he removed his t-shirt and blue jeans, then crawled into his bed and snuggled underneath the sheets. Tonight he would savor the softness of his pillow and the comfort of his mattress. He couldn't say when he would sleep in this bed again.

Chapter 2

EMIKO SAT AMONG the cool green trees and bushes that surrounded Frontier View, toeing the line between the forest and the clearing. Adults worked in gardens nearby, digging potatoes from the ground and picking not-quite-ripe tomatoes from their vines. A group of kids played in the tall grass of the village square, throwing a ball back and forth. Emiko wondered how children — some even older than herself — could continue to play and play such childish games all day long.

From her hiding place in the shadows, safe from the heat of late summer, Emiko watched as a light wind carried white dandelion seeds through the air. They hovered above the clearing like wispy, thumb-sized ghosts, uncertain of which direction to fly. Like all things in Frontier View, they were peaceful. Too peaceful.

Emiko turned her attention to the day's main event. In the distance, her brother Nathan packed and readied a wagon with the help of the ever-mysterious, ever-bearded John Osborne — or Beard, as she liked to call him. Cynthia, Pierre, and a few other villagers had gathered to watch as the two men made their final preparations, double-checking their provisions.

Why did she even bother watching them pack? Though she wanted to join the expedition to Mallard Island, she already knew what the answer would be if she asked again: a resounding "No." Emiko could shoot, track, and live off the gifts of the forest — better than her brother, even — and yet Beard had chosen to take Nathan, not her. Never in her fourteen years had any decision seemed so unfair.

Despite her frustration, Emiko watched the preparations intently. Beard and Nathan circled their cart, making sure that the canoe and other gear were strapped down tightly. The cart was pulled by Mumford, the hardiest of Frontier View's tvapas. As was typical of tvapas, Mumford had the head and black-and-white hide of a Holstein but the body and antlers of a wild Minnesota moose.

Emiko looked on as Nathan spoke to Beard. Nathan then jogged towards the cabin he shared with her. Beard strode over to chat with Pierre. He started conversing, patting the revolver on his hip. Pierre nodded eagerly, putting a hand on Mumford's back. As their conversation continued, Emiko imagined it aloud, creating her own version of their dialogue.

"Don't worry, Pierre. I'll take good care of Nathan. I know he's like a son to you," she said to herself in a deep, gruff voice.

"Oh, I'm not worried. Why, I'm glad you can show him the world! He's grown so much in these last few weeks since you've come to Frontier View," she continued the mock conversation in a friendly, singsong voice.

"By the way, I've been thinking I should bring Emiko along as well."

"Oh, is that right? Well, I think that's a stupendous idea! She's the greatest sharpshooter Frontier View has ever seen. Why, I heard she once hit a mosquito from three hundred yards out, while blindfolded, no less! In fact, it's a truly amazing story ..."

"Sorry, Pierre, but I don't have time for another of your stories. If I hear one more my ears will fall off."

"Ha! I've never let that stop me before, and I'm certainly not going to let it stop me —"

"Emiko! What are you doing back there?" Nathan's voice broke into her reverie. "Are you talking to yourself?"

Emiko let out an exasperated grunt. She swept the underbrush aside and stepped out into the sunlight.

"I was just enjoying a little peace and quiet in the shade," she said, rolling her eyes. "Seems like the whole town is oohing and aahing over this grand adventure you and Beard are leaving on."

"Loons over the moon, Emiko — are you ever going to let up? I don't get why you keep hassling me about it. You know it wasn't my decision. Did you see how much talking Pierre had to do with John to convince him to even take me along?"

"But then why you and not me?"

Nathan glared at her and let out a groan of frustration. "Will you at least come and say goodbye?"

With a harrumph, Emiko crossed her arms and swung her head to avert her eyes from Nathan. Her long black hair glistened as it danced in the sunlight.

"Suit yourself," Nathan said. He trudged back to meet Beard and the rest of the group.

Why can't he ever see things from my point of view? Emiko wondered, biting her lower lip. She ran her hand over the stock of the lightweight Ruger 10/22 rifle slung across her back. *So much for going hunting this morning.*

Reluctantly, she walked over to the group surrounding the wagon to say farewell. She owed Beard that much.

"Are you sure you have everything you need?" Pierre said with a cheerful smile.

"Yeah, I'm sure," Beard replied.

"You put the money I gave you in a safe place? I know it's not much, but it's all we can manage. We don't have much use for money here in Frontier View."

"Yeah, the Minnesota dollars are tucked away safely in my pack." Beard reached a hand out to Pierre and the two men shared a firm handshake. "Thanks for all of your help."

"No, thank you, John. We can't begin to repay you for the assistance you've given us." Pierre withdrew his hand. "Take good care of Nathan, now," he added.

Beard nodded, his expression calm. Emiko rolled her eyes, annoyed at the countless times she'd heard Pierre make that request.

"And Nathan," Pierre said, addressing her brother. "Listen and learn from John, and do what you can to be of help."

"Sure thing!" Nathan said with an eager nod.

"And remember that no matter where you go, Frontier View will always be here, awaiting your return." Pierre's eyes beamed with pride from behind his horn-rimmed glasses. He offered his hand for a shake. Nathan, however, brushed the gesture aside and gave Pierre a big hug instead.

"Don't worry, I'll be back before you know it."

Emiko was next. Nathan stepped forward and threw his arms around her. She didn't refuse, but merely let her arms hang limp at her sides. "I'll miss you, Emiko," he said, releasing her from his embrace. She had nothing to say in reply.

"You ready to go, kid?" Beard asked Nathan.

"Yeah, let's move on out," Nathan replied. He stepped in front of Mumford and tugged on the rope attached to the beast's harness, urging him to pull ahead.

Emiko watched her brother go, thinking back to the last time she'd seen him leave town. It had been nearly a year since then, when he'd gone to Duluth together with their father only to return alone.

Emiko felt a hand on her shoulder, yanking her mind back to the present. Beard stood before her.

"Hey, huntress," he said. "Keep practicing with that pea-shooter of yours. Your opportunity will come, sooner than you think. The world can always use another self-sufficient sharpshooter." He smiled gently at her, his lips partially obscured by his scruffy beard. Releasing his hand from her shoulder, he turned to catch up with Nathan and the cart.

"Think they'll be alright?" Cynthia said, gazing at the two men and the cart as they rapidly shrank from view.

"I'm sure of it," Pierre replied.

"Just the same, I'll miss having a big, strong man like him around."

"You mean Nathan, right?" Pierre grinned.

Cynthia drew her eyebrows together. "Pierre, you know who I mean."

"Indeed. I'm happy for the two of you."

"So am I." She smiled. "Hopefully it won't be the last I see of him."

"Both he and Nathan will return. Of that much I'm certain."

When the two men and their cart reached the edge of the forest, Nathan turned back and raised his open hand high above his head, making a final gesture of farewell. Pierre, Cynthia, and the rest of the townsfolk waved in return.

Emiko gazed at the cart as it rounded the bend and disappeared behind the cover of the woods. Having lost sight of her brother and Beard, she moped away from the crowd, back into the forest. There, behind the cover of the trees, she rested on a large tree stump.

They were gone. She was losing both Beard and Nathan, the two men who had just rescued her from a grim fate. In that moment of silent reflection, Emiko swore to herself that one day, soon, she would return the favor.

Chapter 3

LATER THAT EVENING Emiko sat in Pierre's one-room cabin, watching as Pierre tended the red hot coals in the wood stove. The old man poked and prodded to evenly distribute the heat for cooking. A metal tray on the table in front of Emiko held two rabbits and a ruffed grouse, all skillfully skinned and butchered.

"We're gonna become carnivores while Nathan is away, aren't we," Emiko grumbled. "I'll miss the potatoes and greens he always brought home."

"Don't forget, we'll still have my share of the village garden," Pierre called back as he continued to tend the stove.

"But it won't be enough for the two of us."

Pierre craned his neck to look at Emiko. "Hmm ..." he said, pursing his lips as he nodded thoughtfully.

"Couldn't we trade some of my wild game for vegetables?" Emiko asked.

"Well, I'm afraid most people in Frontier View enjoy eating ruffed grouse, squirrel, and rabbit about as much as you do. I don't imagine we could bring back enough veggies in a trade to make it worth our while," Pierre said, his face grim.

With a sigh, Emiko hopped from her seat, took the tray of meat, and set it beside the cast-iron stove. She placed a frying pan on the stove top, poured a thin layer of water into the bottom from one of Pierre's ceramic jugs, and then tossed the chunks of meat into the water.

"You really should let the water heat up a bit before you add the meat," Pierre said.

Emiko shrugged. "It'll taste gamy either way."

"Maybe you could spend some time in the garden, Emiko. It'd be a good solution to our dilemma and a good experience for you, as well."

"Me? Gardening? No way!"

"Suit yourself. If you get ever sick of being a carnivore, you can always change your mind."

Pierre stirred the reddish-brown chunks of meat in the pan with a big wooden spoon. The water in the pan began to bubble. Emiko watched in silence, entranced by the simmering meat.

"Say, Emiko, you aren't too disappointed that you couldn't join Nathan and John, are you?"

Emiko rolled her eyes. "Me? Disappointed? *Never.*"

Pierre smirked. "You'll get over it. You're still young and I'm sure you'll have many adventures of your own before long. In the meantime I have a gift for you, something to assuage your frustration a wee bit."

"Oh?" Emiko's eyes lit up in anticipation. She didn't know what assuage meant, but Pierre's tone suggested it was a good thing.

"Patience, Emiko. I'll give it to you after dinner."

Gradually, the water in the frying pan evaporated, leaving a thick, gravy-like residue that added much needed moisture to the gamy rabbit meat. Pierre sprinkled a few flakes of parsley and a smidgen of basil into the pan, then gently stirred, letting the flavors pervade the concoction. Lifting the pan from the stove top, he declared the meal ready.

Emiko quickly set the table, then watched as Pierre distributed the food onto their plates. After returning the pan to a cooler section of the stove top, he sat at the table and beckoned Emiko to do the same.

"Dinner prayer?" he offered.

"Since when do you pray?" Emiko asked.

"I haven't in years. Maybe decades," Pierre said with an easy smile. "But it couldn't hurt to say a few good words for our friends who just set out on the road."

Emiko closed her eyes and waited for Pierre to speak. After clearing his throat, the old man began his prayer.

"I don't know who's listening. In fact, I doubt anyone is listening besides my dear friend Emiko here, not that I'll let that stop me.

"First, I'd like to say that despite all the heartache and pain the Desolation caused, I'm truly grateful that we've been given a fresh chance at life and this opportunity to see the world we once knew in a whole new light. We'll continue to be grateful, until the time comes when we too join our friends and family among the ranks of the departed.

"Second, I want to take a moment to pray for the safety of our good friends, Nathan and John. May they find what they seek and return to us with haste, carried by the wings of expedience. Amen."

"Amen," Emiko repeated, taking her fork and picking at the meat. "Um, by the way, what are the 'wings of expedience'?"

Pierre smiled. "Just the kind of thing an old guy like me tosses in to add a little spark to his speaking."

Emiko made a face, but decided not to pursue the point any further, instead focusing on her meal. After absent-mindedly cutting her meat into bite sized pieces, she looked up and noticed that Pierre was giving her a questioning stare, squinting at her through his thick horn-rimmed glasses.

"Pierre, is something wrong?"

"No — nothing wrong," he said, his expression softening. "I just hope I'm not jumping the gun, so to speak."

Emiko furrowed her brow, returning to her meal. She ate methodically, placing the chunks of meat in her mouth piece by piece. It had a strong, wild taste, but the basil and parsley garnishes provided a welcome dash of flavor.

Her plate was soon clean. Emiko pushed it toward the center of the table and quietly waited for Pierre to finish. He always ate slowly, taking time to appreciate every last bite. Once he'd had his fill, Pierre stood up and stepped over to a closet near his bed. From her chair, Emiko watched as the white-haired man opened the door and pulled out a long dark object.

A rifle.

Is that for me? Emiko wondered. She'd been begging for a new rifle for months. Why was he giving her one now?

Pierre carefully closed the closet and returned to the table, wearing a disconcerted expression.

"Your father told me to entrust this weapon to you when I felt you were ready," he said. "It's an M1903 Springfield. Are you familiar with it?"

"No, but I will be soon!" Emiko said, bounding from of her chair and eagerly approaching Pierre to examine the gift. The rifle looked gorgeous. Its stock and body were both crafted from dark wood, with only a short nub of metal, the barrel, protruding from the front end.

"Walnut stock. Shoots .30-06 rounds. A classic rifle used in the biggest wars of our time, from World War I to Vietnam. Looks original, save for the aftermarket scope. I don't know where your father, Ryota, came upon it, or where he kept it hidden, but when he was nearing the end he entrusted it to me for safekeeping until you were ready," Pierre said.

"Not to Nathan?" Emiko asked.

Pierre shook his head. "Nathan has many strengths, but I think we can all agree that you're the better marksman."

At that, Emiko wrapped her arms around the old man.

"Easy now," Pierre exclaimed with a grunt, shifting his grip on the rifle. "You might break a bone or two in this old body."

After Emiko relaxed her embrace, Pierre held the rifle in his open palms and presented it to her. She put her hands under the rifle, and for a moment the two held it together.

"Remember, Emiko, this isn't a toy — it's a real weapon. Be mindful of that fact and use it wisely," Pierre said, retracting his hands.

"Thank you," Emiko said, appreciating the heft of the rifle in her hands. It was heavier than her Ruger 10/22. She was sure it had far more stopping power, as well. "What about ammunition?" she asked.

"I believe it will accept most kinds of .30-06 rounds. Guns from this era weren't as finicky as more recent varieties."

"Great. I think have some sitting around my house."

"*Your* house?" Pierre chuckled. "Seems you've forgotten about your brother already."

Emiko grinned slyly. "Don't worry — I haven't forgotten." After thoroughly examining the rifle, she rested it against the wall and began to clear the dishes from the table.

* * *

As soon as she'd finished helping Pierre tidy up the dining area, Emiko left the old man's cabin and returned home. She wanted to wake up early the next morning to test out the rifle. After slipping out of her shirt and khakis she flopped onto bed. Resting on the quilt, she stared up at the ceiling.

I can hunt anything now, Emiko thought. The Springfield could take down big game such as moose and deer, though she would need help carrying the meat back to the village. She was also now better equipped to defend herself against the predators of the forest if the need arose. She hoped it wouldn't.

Through her open bedroom window she heard a pair of men talking outside. Their conversation jumped from the weather to crops to moonshine and everything in between. Listening to them only served to remind her that while her brother was out exploring the world, she was stuck in Frontier View. She'd come to this village when she was very young and had never left, never ventured farther than a day or two away. So much time had passed that she could barely remember her birthplace, Minneapolis.

She thought back to those final weeks of the Desolation, when her mother had died. Though Emiko hadn't understood at the time, her father had expected they would all die together. He'd believed they would all pass quietly, together as a family. Fortunately, things didn't quite work out that way. As it happened, her father had been immune to the Desolation virus, and he'd passed that immunity on to his two children. At a time when billions had died, they'd been spared.

After surviving their first winter in Minneapolis, which had become a sprawling ghost town of empty malls and abandoned homes, her family had journeyed north with Pierre and others. Eventually, they'd settled in the area that she now called home — Frontier View.

Frontier View was home, but was it supposed to be her home forever?

It couldn't be. It wouldn't be.

The talking outside had stopped. Emiko rolled out of bed and looked out the window. Lamplight still flickered in a few of the village's cabins. She threw herself back onto her bed and impatiently gazed at the unlit ceiling. Time drifted past, the minutes ticking by slowly, like a moose lazily lunching in the marsh.

Eventually, Emiko rose from bed again and put on her khakis and green shirt. She grabbed her backpack from the corner of the main room and began to load it with gear. She stuffed the pack with clothes, a small tent, a sleeping bag, a map of Minnesota, a hatchet, and a few other odds and ends. Knowing the ways of the forest, she could afford to pack light.

She eyed her Ruger 10/22, leaning against the wall. *Sorry, old friend,* she thought, *but you're going to have to stay here.* In her closet, she found a cache of .30-06 rounds that her father had left behind. She deposited the ammunition in a small rucksack. After carefully placing the rucksack in her backpack, she slid the butt of the Springfield rifle into one of the pack's side compartments and tightly cinched two straps to secure it.

She peered out a window. All of the other cabins were dark. The stars were out and the moon was a few slivers shy of full. Content that it was a good night for travel, she made for the door.

Halfway out the door, she stopped and turned back. If she was going to do this, she needed to consider the people she was leaving behind. She found a piece of paper and a pencil and wrote a note, addressing it to Pierre. He wouldn't be pleased but Emiko hoped maybe, just maybe, he would understand.

When she'd finished the note, she set it on the kitchen table. Her heart raced as she struck off resolutely into the night. Though she didn't have a concrete plan, she intended to follow Beard and Nathan to see if she could help them.

An adventure of her own making awaited.

Chapter 4

RAMSES SLOUCHED in his swivel chair, surrounded on all sides by unpainted concrete walls. Before him were two tables, their tops littered with every manner of radio equipment. The tables formed an 'L' against the back corner of the tiny room. He rested one arm on each table as he took a deep breath through his nose, letting the dry, stale air tickle his nostrils.

He'd endured a lot in the past few weeks: a shoot-out with John Osborne, an encounter with that mysterious woman in red, and finally a harried trek back to Restoration Army HQ, a journey made in part on a horse he'd requisitioned.

He'd been assigned this post in the Restoration Army's central communications room because he'd earned the General's trust, and because the General wanted to give him time to recuperate. Unfortunately, the tedium did not sit well with Ramses. Sometimes hours went by without any radio activity, leaving him with nothing to do but tap his fingers on the desk and dream of being reassigned. His first encounter with John Osborne had left him nerve-wracked but hungry for more action.

A red light blinked on his radio console, signaling an outgoing transmission — a transmission from the General himself. The lone perk of working in the comm room was that Ramses had clearance to listen to most of the Army's radio chatter. Ramses picked the bulky headset up from the table and slid it over his ears.

"Yeah, this is Lieutenant Bogues, Pickerel Lake Outpost, speaking." The man's voice warbled slightly through the heavy static, the signal having been boosted by numerous radio repeaters.

"Lieutenant Bogues, this is the General." His voice rang clearly through Ramses' headset.

"Howdy, sir. What's the good word?"

"The 'good word,' Lieutenant?"

"Just trying to lighten the mood, sir. Why the call?"

The General paused before answering. *Will he really let a subordinate get away with using that kind of language, especially when he knows I might be listening?* Ramses wondered.

"I have a job for you, Lieutenant. I've received reports of a suspicious entity snooping around your section of our territory. We suspect she's heading to —

"Did I hear you say 'she'?"

"Yes, Lieutenant, she. Is that important?"

"Just had to confirm what kind of pie I'm dipping my fingers into, sir."

The General paused again before continuing.

"We suspect she's heading to Mallard Island on Rainy Lake to rendezvous with another high priority target of ours. She should pass by your outpost, traveling alone along the Trans-Canada Highway, sometime within the next few days."

"Another high priority target?"

"I'll tell you more about that at the proper time, Lieutenant."

The lieutenant gave a haughty snort. "Alright. What's the deal with this gal?"

"I want you to follow her."

"Sounds like a good job for one of our new recruits. I'll send one of the youngsters after her."

I'd kill to have that job, yet he just brushes it off like it's nothing? Ramses thought with a frown. He had given the General the initial report of this "suspicious entity" — a woman in a red sweatshirt with a strange tattoo — only to be rewarded with the dullest assignment within the Restoration Army's ranks.

"No, Lieutenant," the General continued. "You'll handle this personally. The subject is armed and potentially dangerous. I need your skills and experience."

"I got plenty of both, boss. What's her profile?" the lieutenant's voice crackled through the radio.

"Young, brown hair, wears a red sweater, carries a revolver, has a small tattoo on her wrist."

"Is that all you got?"

"Lieutenant, how many people matching that description have passed by your outpost?"

"Approximately zero."

The General offered no response. Radio static dutifully filled the gap in the conversation. Ramses wondered who would speak next.

The lieutenant broke the silence. "I see your point. So, you just want me to follow her?"

"For now, yes."

"Roger that. I'll keep watch for her." The lieutenant cleared his voice with a cough. "By the way, sir, are we gonna get a fresh delivery of supplies soon? Herbal cigarettes are alright, but I got a hankerin' for nicotine."

"I didn't muster the Restoration Army to serve as your personal tobacco plantation, Lieutenant. However, I'll see what I can do."

"Much appreciated. I'll keep an eye out for this Suzie Q. I won't let you down, sir."

"Glad to hear it, Lieutenant Bogues. The General, over and out."

Ramses tilted his head and rubbed the back of his neck. Did the General really allow such insolence to fester within his ranks? As Ramses pondered the question, the General's voice broke through his headphones.

"Private Brushnell, do you copy?"

"Yes, sir," Ramses answered reflexively, startled by the call.

"The General, speaking. I trust you overheard my conversation with Lieutenant Bogues."

"Correct, sir."

"What did you think about his manner of speaking?"

Ramses hesitated. Why was the General asking his opinion?

"Permission to speak freely, sir."

"Granted."

"His speech bordered on insubordination, sir. If I spoke to you that way, I doubt I'd live to see the setting sun."

"Astute, Private Brushnell. Next question: Do you know how Lieutenant Bogues attained his rank?"

"I do not, sir."

"Lieutenant Bogues and I have a history, a history that goes back to our time together in the U.S. Marine Corps. When forming the Restoration Army, it was useful to assign higher positions to men whom I knew well. However, I'm not one to let my officers rest on their laurels, and I'm not afraid to strip an officer of his rank. I want to build a force where ambition and dedication are rewarded, not seniority and cronyism."

"Is that a warning, sir?"

"Not a warning, Private. A statement of purpose." The General cleared his throat. "I appreciate all of the information you've provided regarding Osborne and our mysterious woman. Continue on your current trajectory, and I see a future for you in the ranks of my officers. "

"Thank you, sir."

"In the meantime, let's consider Lieutenant Bogues' assignment a test. If he proves his worth to me, I'll treat his unrefined remarks with leniency."

"And if not, sir?"

"A man reaps what he sows." The General paused, giving his words time to sink in. "Keep up the good work, Private. The General, over and out."

The radio fell silent. Ramses removed his headset, wondering if the General trusted him more than he'd imagined. In any case, if a clash between John Osborne, Lieutenant Bogues, and the red-clad woman was brewing, Ramses would keep tabs on the situation with interest.

Chapter 5

ARISTOTLE WALKED briskly along the Trans-Canada Highway, thru the Indian grass, chicory, and Queen Anne's lace that shot up from the cracks in the pavement. Above, puffy white cumulus clouds drifted across the pale blue sky.

The Desolation had taught Aristotle how to live alone, yet never had she felt more alone than now. The highway cut through the dense forests of southern Ontario like a bridge across a vast, endless body of water. The nearest human settlement — and, by extension, the nearest living soul — could've been hundreds of kilometers away.

Griswold had told her to find out more about the General. She'd had no luck until a week ago, when she'd encountered the young, blonde-haired soldier at the General's outpost. He'd told her that the General and John Osborne were working together. This left her with a choice: keep on the General's trail or track down Osborne. Though she suspected the two diverging trails would eventually rejoin, Aristotle could follow only one at a time.

The opportunity to discover what Osborne was up to proved the greater temptation. Were Osborne truly working for the General, Aristotle's curiosity and pride demanded that she know the how and why. And so here she was, trekking down the lonesome wilderness highway.

The hours passed slowly, one plodding step at a time. Eventually, a side road materialized in the distance. A corroded green metal sign indicated that the town of Atikokan was three kilometers down the diverging road.

Did she have time for a side trip? Diverging from her path would cost her a couple of hours. If the town had useful information, it would be time well spent. She curled her fingers around the straps of her backpack and quickened her pace. Even if she found what she wanted, it would be of no use if she didn't make it to Mallard Island in time to catch Osborne.

Her brisk pace quickly carried her to the outskirts of the town. After enduring days of unbroken wilderness, the sight of the village cheered her. On the right shoulder of the road a sign welcomed her to Atikokan, population 2842. Considering that less than two percent of the humans had possessed the viral immunity, Aristotle figured that of those 2842 people, thirty to forty had survived the Desolation. She doubted that those few survivors had stuck around in the wake of the viral onslaught.

Her stroll through the village quickly reinforced her prediction. Just like every other abandoned town she'd passed through, Atikokan could only be described as oddly and unnervingly tranquil. Where shingles and siding had fallen off the houses, moss and vines had grown to replace them. Where human bones slowly decayed, other creatures had come to make use of the man-made shelters that yet stood. Where the virus had brought death, it had laid the groundwork for new life.

The human toll went far beyond the immediate death count. Those not felled by the scourge lived with an unholy mixture of loneliness, despair, and survivor guilt. Suicide was commonplace. Aristotle's sister, Isabel, had been one such case.

After watching their mother die, Isabel had decided to end her life before the virus could claim her. What she hadn't known was that she may have been immune to the virus. The immunity ran in families. The fact that Aristotle possessed it meant Isabel would've had a fifty-fifty chance of having it as well.

Isabel had squandered that chance, leaving Aristotle forever guilty of not protecting and supporting her sister. The knowledge that her sister could possibly still be here, alive, hung over Aristotle's days like a rain cloud blotting out the sun.

Left with the choice to wallow in her sorrow and guilt or use it as motivation to move forward, Aristotle had chosen the latter. Where she found injustice, she strove to eliminate it. Though she couldn't bring her sister back, she could try to make the world a better place for those who lived on. She'd made improving the world her personal mandate, and that objective had served her well through the post-Desolation years.

Aristotle continued roaming the streets of the small town. Before long, she found what she'd been looking for — the Atikokan Public Library. Despite the foliage clinging to the building's concrete exterior, the library appeared to have weathered the seasons well.

Aristotle let herself in through the unlocked front door. She proceeded down the entry corridor, accompanied by the muffled sound of her rubber soles against the decaying carpet. At the end of the entryway she passed through a second set of doors, into the library proper. Sunlight from large bay windows enveloped the room in an eerie glow. Specks of dust flitted through the broad streams of light. The room reeked of musk and mildew. Aristotle hoped the mold hadn't spread to the books.

She walked past the front desk, towards the extensive collection of books. She gave the shelves of fiction and children's titles a cursory glance before making her way to the non-fiction section, intent on finding information about Mallard Island and Rainy Lake.

The books she required would be located in the geography and history sections. Aristotle weaved back and forth through the dust-caked aisles, gently sliding her fingers along the outer edges of the hardwood shelves. Though she enjoyed reading, she realized that she wasn't familiar with how libraries organized their non-fiction.

After browsing the shelves for a time, she came across the history section. She scanned for books about Minnesota history. When a title on the top shelf caught her eye, she stood on her tiptoes to wiggle it free from its neighbors.

A crashing sound rang throughout the room. Releasing the book, Aristotle reached for her revolver and spun around. Both hands clenched the bulky gun tightly, holding it before her, ready to fire.

She carefully paced back toward the entrance, toward the source of the sound. Her heart thumped, her racing pulse reverberating in her ears. She cautiously poked her head out from the rows of books, her eyes darting back and forth as she surveyed the room.

She stepped out from the cover of the shelves. On the ground, near the children's books, she spotted a shattered vase. Keeping her gun at the ready, she ventured closer and knelt over the ceramic shards.

Was someone else in the library with her? The hairs on her arms stood erect at the thought. She drew short, labored breaths, struggling to remain silent.

"Meowwwwwww."

Aristotle's eyes shot toward the corner of the room. A pair of wide, penetrating eyes stared back at her from the shadows.

"Meowwwww," the cat called out again. Aristotle squinted, picking out the animal from its surroundings. It had a slender body, covered by a white and brown calico coat.

Returning her revolver to its holster, Aristotle let out a sigh of relief. As she rose to her feet, the feral cat darted off, silently disappearing behind a collection of Blu-ray cases.

The cat had looked young. Though she couldn't say for sure, Aristotle guessed that it was the offspring of a former pet. Many house cats and dogs had died when their owners had succumbed to the Desolation virus. Many others had rediscovered their wild instincts. They had learned to fend for themselves and now often made their homes and raised their families in buildings that humans had abandoned.

Aristotle returned to the history section and slid the book she'd wanted out from the shelf, a volume entitled *Mallard in the Rain: The Life and Times of Ernest Oberholtzer*. On the cover was a picture of a vigorous old man, paddling a canoe across an open body of water. The back cover indicated that it was about the relationship between Mallard Island and Ernest Oberholtzer, the man who'd once called the island home. Aristotle set her pack on the ground, unzipped it, and slid the thick paperback inside. The library wouldn't miss the book, and the information inside would give her a better idea of what she would encounter on the island.

As she made her way toward the exit, Aristotle detected a subtle movement. She stopped in front of the checkout desk, gazing out the window behind it. She could've sworn she'd seen a shadow sweeping across the tall, wild blades of grass outside.

She hurried out the library's front entrance and circled once around the building, taking care as she turned each corner. *Strange*, she thought when she found nothing, shaking her head. She noticed that her shadow had grown long in the late afternoon sun. The shadows of the forest denizens would've grown long, as well. Perhaps that was what she'd seen.

Aristotle tightened the straps of her pack and broke into a trot, heading back in the direction from which she had come. Soon she found herself at the outskirts of the village. When would another traveler visit the desolate little town? Months, maybe years, could pass before Atikokan would see another soul. She mulled over that thought as she hurried toward the Trans-Canada Highway, eager to make it back before nightfall.

Chapter 6

MUMFORD, THE HARDIEST of tvapas, trudged steadily ahead, pulling his burden south along the uneven pavement of Minnesota Highway 61. The wheels of the cart rumbled over the bulges and fissures in the blacktop. The road, now nine years of harsh winters and steamy summers removed from any form of maintenance, had seen better days.

Alongside the pack animal marched Nathan and John. To their left was Lake Superior, an expanse of shimmering blue so wide that it could've passed for the ocean. To their right was the Superior National Forest, the lush northern jungle which Nathan and John were leaving behind, at least for the time being.

Already it was the fourth day of their journey toward Duluth. Much to the travelers' good fortune the weather had so far been pleasant. They enjoyed the calls of the birds by day and the calm lapping of the waves by night, and each day when the sun rose they awoke to the misty air and the sight of dew clinging to the wild grass.

The uneventful days of walking grew long. Nathan occupied his mind by kicking the pebbles and stones he found along the pavement. He would follow one until he accidentally knocked it off the road into the overgrowth, and then move on to another. Eventually, when yet another of his stones rolled off the pavement with no suitable replacement in sight, Nathan tried another tact to stave off the boredom of travel.

"John?"

"Yeah?"

"Mind if I ask you something?"

"Shoot."

Nathan scratched at the back of his neck. "Why don't you ever talk about yourself?"

"What do you want to hear?"

"I don't know," Nathan said. "Anything. Like, what did you do after the Desolation struck?"

John didn't reply, keeping his eyes trained on the southern horizon. As the gentle Lake Superior waves rolled in and out of the rocky shore in the backdrop, Nathan saw a pair of bushy-tailed squirrels dart across the dark pavement in the distance.

"John?" Nathan tried again.

"It's complicated," John said.

"Complicated?"

"I told you I was in a hospital, out cold during that time, right?"

"Yeah, I remember," Nathan said. "So?"

John heaved a sigh through his nose. "I was in a hospital for eight years, unconscious"

"Eight years!" Nathan exclaimed. He moved to cover his mouth, embarrassed by his outburst.

"Right," John said. "You wanna hear the story or not?"

"Of course I wanna hear it" Nathan nodded.

John took a moment to collect his thoughts before beginning.

"It began in 2026. That's when I lost my arm in Egypt while serving in the U.S. Marine Corps. That's the last thing I remember before the Desolation," John said.

"Why were you in Egypt?"

"I was mopping up after a geopolitical crisis. The kind of thing that bubbled up every few years back in the day."

Nathan nodded. "We lived in a different world then."

"Yeah." John nodded in agreement. "Anyway, when I woke up I was in an underground hospital. I remembered I'd lost my arm, so I was surprised to find a new one grafted to my left shoulder." John reached across his body and massaged the joint where his bionic arm was attached. "The hospital was empty — no people, no sound. No one to tell me how long I'd been out of commission or what the deal with my arm was. The only thing that gave me a sense of how much time had passed was the length of my beard. It had grown so long that there could have been mice nesting in it. So, the first thing I did was find a scissors and cut it short."

Nathan rubbed his chin. "Like it is now?"

"Like it is now. Same for my hair." John ran a hand through his short, dark hair. "After taking care of that, I turned my thoughts to escaping. Getting out of that underground facility was more trouble than fixing a broken trigger, but eventually I managed to make it topside. Once I'd busted out, I could see immediately that I wasn't in Egypt anymore. I figured I was somewhere in the northern United States or maybe Europe. I started wandering around. Before long I determined that I was in the U.S., but something was wrong. Very wrong."

"I can only imagine," Nathan said, shaking his head. "Minneapolis was quiet and empty after the Desolation, but at least I understood what had happened."

"Must've been a rough time for you, too," John said.

"Yeah, but I had my father and sister with me," Nathan said. "Anyway, go on."

"I drifted aimlessly for a few days, passing all the empty houses and abandoned cars. That continued until one afternoon, when I came across an old, white-haired man sitting behind the counter of a Shell station. I rushed in and asked him where the hell I was and what the hell had happened."

"He didn't realize you had been out so long," Nathan said.

"Of course. He didn't understand my situation. How could he? He stared at me for a long while before he spoke. You know what the first thing he said to me was? He said, 'You forgot to shave. That's what happened.'"

"A clean shave is what separates man from the beasts, it's said." Nathan raised his palms defensively, holding them between himself and John. "No offense."

"None taken. Anyhow, after hearing that nugget of wisdom I just stared back at him, rubbing my beard. We stared at each other for a long time, neither of us batting an eyelid."

"Who broke first?"

"He did. He asked me why I was wearing army fatigues. I told him I'd just woken up in the military hospital down south and had no idea where the hell I was. He didn't look convinced

— said he didn't know of a hospital down south. Fortunately, though, he didn't get too hung up on that point. He grilled me a bit more after that, but before long he told me I looked like a tough son of a bitch and offered me a drink. I accepted, he pulled out a bottle of whiskey, and we got to it. Once he heard my story he lightened up a bit. He told me where I was — Northern Maine — and then continued on about everything that'd happened, the Desolation and whatnot."

"So, they call it the Desolation in Maine, too?" Nathan asked.

"Yeah. I've heard it called a few other things in my travels, but usually it's 'the Desolation.'"

"Then what happened?"

"Turns out he was ex-military, an Iraq war veteran. He'd lost his family and was living alone in the gas station, making ends meet by scavenging, hunting, and fishing. Not many people passed through his part of the world, he said. I'd been the first in nearly half a year."

Nathan nodded, wondering what it would feel like to live alone instead of in a community like Frontier View. The winters would be rough, especially when the snow and ice grew heavy. A man living on his own would have a difficult time preparing enough food to last the winter, and would have to rely on his hunting skills — a risky proposition, given the unpredictable weather.

"Anyway, the couple days I'd spent drifting across Maine had given me a taste of the new world, and the old guy's explanation made it clear that there was nothing left for me on the eastern seaboard. So the next morning I said goodbye and continued north."

"Why north?" Nathan asked.

"Fewer people and less civilization. I figured wandering through the wilderness would be less depressing than passing through empty cityscapes. Also, the old man told me that before the virus struck, nukes had gone off in a handful of major cities. I wanted to avoid the radioactive fallout."

"Also, you know, your beard makes you look like a lumberjack," Nathan volunteered. "A perfect fit for the north."

John furrowed his brow.

"Sorry," Nathan apologized. "So, how did you end up in Minnesota?"

"By accident, mostly. I had a run-in with a wannabe cop in Ontario and decided to hightail it out of there. I ended up crossing back stateside, into Minnesota."

"What were things like in Ontario?"

"Toronto is rebuilding nicely, but outside of the city it's pretty much the Wild West. Not unlike here."

"Wait until you see Duluth. It's the capital of the Republic of Minnesota, and it's where they print Minnesota dollars, like the ones Pierre gave us."

"Where are the boundaries of Minnesota?"

Nathan shrugged. "Kind of up in the air. Man-made borders quickly lose meaning when most of the men die. The representatives in the statehouse probably have tentative borders drawn up, but I couldn't tell you what they look like."

"Politics," John muttered. "Say, have you been to Duluth before?"

"Yeah." Nathan looked down at his shoes. His last trip to Duluth hadn't been a pleasant one, and he didn't much like talking about it, not even with Pierre. It struck him that discussing one's past wasn't always easy, a fact that probably held true for John, as well.

As the hours passed the sun sank lower and lower, continuing its descent toward trees along the western horizon, and hues of red and orange gradually began to seep into the cloudless azure sky. Nathan could make out a faint sound in the distance, like the roaring engine of a car speeding down the highway. The sound grew louder, drawing closer.

Nathan squinted, gazing down the long strip of pavement. He opened his eyes wide, stunned by the sight of an object zooming south along the shoreline — a black car. Hastily, Nathan ordered Mumford to the side of the road, unsure of how the driver would react to a cart and tvapa in the middle of the road.

The car, failing to slow down, honked as it approached. A rush of air whooshed through Nathan's hair as the car swerved to avoid the cart.

"You know your cars?" John asked as he watched the car speed into the distance. The vehicle became a black speck before disappearing completely.

Nathan shook his head.

"That was a Honda Civic, an 80s model. About fifty years old by now. I suppose they chose it because it's easy to service — cars had fewer electronics back then — but still gets good gas mileage."

Nathan shrugged. "I'm surprised they managed to find gas. Where do you think they got it?"

"Good question," John said, tapping his finger against his head thoughtfully. "Gas goes bad after a year or two, so it's definitely not fuel leftover from before the Desolation. I imagine there's still plenty of untapped oil in Canada — it could be from up there. I wouldn't be surprised if someone's got a refinery up and running."

Nathan pondered that thought. He'd always assumed he'd never get the chance to drive a car, but the sight of the Honda made him reconsider.

"Still, gas is rare. They probably aren't just up here for fun, wasting fuel. What do you think they're up to?" Nathan asked.

"Your guess is as good as mine."

Nathan let the conversation end there, and John made no attempt to revive it. Soon, before the last rays of sunlight disappeared behind the horizon, the two pulled over to the side of the road, where they set up their A-frame tent and built a blazing campfire.

"Alright, kid, it's my turn to ask a question," John said, as he roasted a skewer of rabbit and squirrel meat over the hot, reddish-gold flames.

"Sure."

"I looked at the map. Passing through Duluth is definitely not the shortest way to International Falls and Mallard Island. This route is taking us west, but we gotta go pretty far south before veering north again. Why didn't we cut straight west on Minnesota Highway 1?"

Nathan shook his head. "Too dangerous. We'd have to pass through Ely, which is deep within Redemption territory."

"Redemption?"

"The people there call themselves the Great Society of the Redemption. They see the Desolation not as a tragic event, but as a chance for mankind to redeem itself. Frontier View had a big dust-up with them and their leader, Mathias West, a few years back. I don't know if they'd give us trouble if we were just passing through, but I'd rather not find out."

"Fair enough. I suppose it's for the best. I'm curious to see what Duluth looks like."

"Well, it's a city, and ..." Nathan said, trailing off as he gazed into the glowing embers. To him, Duluth was a place of suffering and death. He didn't want to delve into that dark corner of his mind tonight. No, this was a chance to enjoy the peaceful sounds of the lake and the forest, and to stare in wonder at the map of stars that would soon appear overhead, illuminating the night sky.

"It's a city ... and?" John prompted.

Nathan sighed, poking at the coals of fire with a stick.

"You'll see for yourself soon enough."

Chapter 7

A WEEK AFTER leaving Frontier View, Beard, Nathan, and Mumford arrived safely in Duluth.

Emiko entered the city not an hour later.

She strode down the middle of the wide street, passing through the suburbs of Duluth. Rows of empty houses lined both shoulders of the pavement, waiting in vain for their owners to return. Though they were larger and more luxurious than the cabins in Frontier View, the houses had seen years of snow, ice, rain, and sun, which had left them with broken windows and fading, peeling paint. Once homes, they were now mere houses — crumbling houses.

Emiko saw now why her family had left Minneapolis to settle in Frontier View. Walking down the streets of Duluth was like walking through a city-sized graveyard. It reminded her of a different era, of a past that she could never return to. Her family had been given a choice: live surrounded by the remains of the Desolation, or find an unsettled corner of the world and start anew. Seeing Duluth, she knew her father had made the right choice for their family. Though Frontier View was small, quiet, and so very unexciting, it had sheltered her from the overwhelming sense of despair and desolation that she now felt.

Her time in Frontier View had also trained her well for the journey she was now making. The adventure thus far had gone smoothly. Though getting a feel for the M1903 Springfield rifle had given her difficultly, once she'd adjusted to its increased stopping power and heavy kick she'd had no trouble bagging game for meals.

Now, however, she was out of her element. The city would present a new set of challenges. Having made it this far, Emiko was confident she could handle any trial that came her way. Gritting her teeth with determination, she walked toward a two-story house, cutting across its weedy, unkempt front lawn. What would she see inside? Corpses? Bones? Or maybe wild animals that had decided to take up residence within?

She stood beside the house's largest window and slowly tilted her head to peek inside. Behind the dirt-smudged glass she saw a living room, complete with a sofa, a pair of fancy chairs, and a television.

Television! The memories of cartoons, movies, and other digital wonders rushed back to her. She felt an urge to run inside and turn on the TV, even though she knew the TV would never power on. She'd lived without electricity for so long that she'd forgotten what it felt like to sit in front of the TV and watch the characters dance around on the screen.

I wonder what other kinds of rooms are inside. She pulled her face away from the mud-streaked windowpane and darted to another. The window she came to was smaller and stood higher off the ground. She lifted her heels so she could see inside.

Her eyes grew wide. A gasp escaped her throat as she stumbled backwards. Inside was a bed with two human skeletons resting upon it. Emiko had seen many corpses in her life — mostly when she'd been much younger — but she'd never seen one from which the flesh was totally gone. She shook her head, calmed her nerves, and took one more look inside the bedroom.

Whoever they were, at least they died together, she thought. Her curiosity satisfied, she returned to the road. The sun was already low in the sky, threatening to fall below the steep hills on the western side of the city.

From her brother's stories, she knew that the city center was where people actually lived. She wanted to make it there before nightfall. She figured Nathan and Beard would spend the night in Duluth, but she still had to determine where they were staying — and do so without being seen.

Emiko moved quickly, taking long strides down the weather-worn pavement, eager to see her first real city since the day her family had left Minneapolis, eight years before.

Chapter 8

AFTER PASSING THROUGH the quiet, lifeless suburbs of Duluth, Nathan and John finally arrived at the city center. In stark contrast to the forlorn, long since abandoned little towns that littered the northern landscape, here in the capital city people wandered the streets, casually examining the many storefronts where Minnesota dollars could be exchanged for goods. Horse drawn carts zipped through the crowds of people, their wooden wheels kicking up dust from the stone pavement.

Though he'd been here once before, Nathan still took in the sights of downtown Duluth with a sense of wonder. It was like no other place he'd seen since the Desolation. He watched with envy as the horses passed, easily pulling ahead of him and Mumford. While the tvapa's ability to subsist on a rugged diet and thrive in the harsh Minnesota winters made him a good fit for Frontier View, walking beside Mumford in the middle of a thriving city like Duluth made Nathan feel like a country bumpkin.

"There's the Republic of Minnesota capitol building." Nathan pointed to a large gray building constructed of wood and stone. "When I came here last year, it was still under construction. Looks like it's finished now."

The capitol was rather quaint by pre-Desolation standards. It stood only two stories tall and was topped by a simple V-shaped roof rather than a dome or a spire. A flight of stone steps led to the entryway, a revolving door flanked on either side by two massive limestone pillars. At the base of the steps stood a sculpture of a black bear, the symbol of the Republic, cast in bronze.

Next to the capitol building was the Bank of Minnesota, where the fledgling republic minted its coins and printed its bills. Though not built with the same level of pain-staking care that had gone into the capitol, the bank was still impressive in its own right. Its exterior was made of bright red bricks, and it had two expansive, glistening windows on either side of a set of dark, imposing hardwood doors.

"How does the government pay for these buildings?" John asked.

"They print money and pay the construction workers with it," Nathan said.

"And that money is accepted throughout Minnesota?"

"For the most part. Most people want to believe in the Republic of Minnesota and are eager to use Minnesota dollars. I think it's especially true here in Duluth, where people can see for themselves that the money is being paid to honest men who are doing quality work."

"So, the value of the cash Pierre gave us is based on faith in the Minnesota government and nothing else?" John rubbed his fingers together, making the gesture for money.

"I think so. I don't quite understand it, either." Nathan shrugged. "Pierre knows a lot more about the subject than I do. He says that Minnesota dollars essentially operate on the same economic principles that currencies have historically been based on."

John took another passing glance at the bank. "Next we have a ransom to pay, I know where I can come to get some quick cash," John said.

"You'd steal from the bank?" Nathan raised an eyebrow.

"Sometimes you gotta do whatever it takes," John replied, with the faintest hint of a smile.

Ahead, Nathan spotted the Lakefront Inn, a two story building lined with dozens of beige doors that led into individual guest rooms. The hotel was in good repair, with cleanly polished windows and what appeared to be a fresh coat of light blue paint on its wooden siding. The parking lot, however, was a different matter. The canoe thumped against the wooden cart as Mumford tugged it toward the hotel lobby. The cart's wheels flattened the wild prairie grass that grew up from the cracks in the blacktop.

The jangle of a bell greeted Nathan as he pulled the lobby door open. Cleanly polished storefront windows allowed sunlight to shine in, naturally illuminating the room. A faded poster hung on the wall, depicting a man and woman lying on a beach, with the catchphrase "Come Say Aloha!" written underneath.

Nathan cocked his head. It had taken them a week to get to Duluth. He couldn't begin to fathom how many months it would take to get to Hawaii.

The front desk remained empty momentarily, until a girl appeared from behind a curtain in the back of the room. She was about the same age as Nathan, a cute brunette. Nathan quickly shifted his gaze so as not to look directly into her eyes.

Nathan glanced back to find John. The bearded man was staring out the window, not paying attention. *I guess he expects me to handle the booking?* Nathan thought, realizing that he'd never dealt with this kind of transaction before.

"Hi there, how may I help you?" the girl asked with a bright smile.

"Um ... we'd like to stay here for a night," Nathan replied, rubbing the back of his neck.

"Sure, we can fix you right up. A room with a pair of twin beds is ten dollars a night."

"Ten dollars? Is that expensive?" Nathan asked earnestly.

The girl let out an amused giggle, revealing a pair of dimples. "I think it's quite a bargain, myself. But then again, I'm probably not the best person to ask."

"Ah, of course," Nathan forced a chuckle. He then looked toward his companion for approval. "John, can we spare ten dollars for a room?"

Without shifting his eyes from the window, John offered a thumbs up.

"We'll take it." Nathan gave a single nod.

"Great. We accept payment in cash only, due at check-in."

"That means now, right?"

"Right." She smiled.

"We left our cash in the cart. I'll go get it."

"It's okay. How about I show you the room, and then you can come back to pay me?" She took a key from underneath the counter and moved for the door. "We'll put you up in Room 107. Follow me." The bell clinked against the glass as she swung the front door open and held it for Nathan and John.

"You first, kid," John said, gesturing for Nathan to exit.

The clerk led them across the parking lot to the row of hotel rooms on the first floor. She walked to the last door and unlocked it.

"You'll be staying here," she said as the door creaked open. "Two beds. No running water, but we do have toilets near the lobby. Just follow the signs. Also, there's a stable above. If you exit the parking lot and walk up the hill around back, you can't miss it. Feel free to hitch your tvapa there. We also have animal feed for sale, should you need it." She placed the room key in Nathan's palm. "Anything else I can do for you?"

"Any good bars in town?" John asked.

"The Drunken Loon is the most popular place in town. Friendly atmosphere, good beer, fair prices. If you leave the parking lot, turn right, and walk a few blocks, you'll find it. You can't miss the sign."

John nodded appreciatively. "Many people staying here tonight?"

"A few. You have neighbors, actually — a couple of men with a car."

"A car?" Nathan jumped in. "John, could it be the same one we saw?"

"Could be." John shrugged.

"It's the first working motor vehicle I've seen in a long while," the hotel clerk offered. "If you saw a car, it's probably the same one. You might bump into the owners at the Drunken Loon. They can't stop talking about much they like the dartboard there." She shot a smile at Nathan. "Anything else I can do for you?"

"No, I think that's all," Nathan replied, looking down at his shoelaces. "Thank you."

"I'll be waiting in the lobby. You can come take care of the bill after you get settled in. I hope you enjoy your stay at the Lakefront Inn." With that she left the room.

Nathan stepped in and sat at the foot of the bed closest to the entrance, immediately noticing the softness of the mattress and the cleanliness of the sheets. Since Duluth was right on Lake Superior, he imagined the residents had figured out a way to use the lake water to help with everyday tasks like bathing and doing laundry. Basic sewer systems could function without electricity.

"Nice place, isn't it?" John asked, leaning against the wall near the entrance.

"Yup," Nathan replied.

"I don't suppose you have many pretty girls your age to talk to in Frontier View, do you?"

"Huh?" Nathan blinked in confusion.

John's lips curved into a half-smile, obscured by his beard. "It's alright. It's a dance we all figure out sooner or later."

"I have no idea what you're talking about, but okay." Nathan stepped toward the door. "I'll go take care of the bill."

"I'll bring in our things." John leaned forward, launching himself off the wall with his shoulder.

Nathan went to get the money from their pack to pay the bill. John, meanwhile, carried their bags into the hotel room, then led Mumford to the stable. After finishing their tasks the two men both returned to the room.

"If it's alright with you, I'm going to walk around the city," Nathan said.

"Go ahead. I'll relax here for a bit, then go see what this place looks like after dark."

"Then I guess I'll either see you back here or go looking for you in the bars."

John nodded. "It's a plan. Enjoy your walk."

Chapter 9

EMIKO MADE HER WAY up a rusty metal ladder, climbing to the rooftop of a four-story lakeside building. Nothing stood between her and the vastness of Lake Superior, adding to the thrill of being so high above the ground. Reaching the top rung, she pulled herself onto the rooftop and turned to admire the lake. Its hard blue surface stretched into the distance, glistening in the afternoon sunlight.

She was safely in downtown Duluth. The journey to Mallard Island was halfway over.

Emiko set down her pack and walked gingerly across the rooftop. From the other side, she watched her brother and Beard check in to the Lakefront Inn.

Compared to what she'd expected, the journey so far had actually been rather tame. Beard and Nathan hadn't required her help. Not that she'd expected they would — they knew how to take care of themselves. Was following them still what she wanted to do? She could continue to do so, and perhaps even reveal that she'd been tailing them since they'd left Frontier View. On the other hand, she was in the big city now. Maybe Duluth would provide her with other avenues for adventure, other ways to make herself useful. Her mind was open to multiple possibilities.

I don't have a place to stay tonight, she realized as she watched Nathan and Beard walk around the hotel parking lot. *But I guess I can always set up my tent somewhere on the outskirts of the city.*

After the two men settled into their room, Emiko saw Nathan leave the hotel and start making his way west, up a steep Duluth hill. Leaving her pack on the rooftop, opting to take only the Springfield rifle, Emiko climbed down the ladder to follow him. Her shoes clanged against the metal rungs as she hurried down.

To make sure Beard wouldn't see her, Emiko jogged around the back of the Lakefront Inn. Rounding the far corner of the building, she then cut back to the street where she'd seen her brother. He was three blocks ahead of her, moving rapidly up the sharply inclined road.

Would he recognize her at this distance? Emiko held back for a few moments, allowing Nathan to gain more ground before following him up the hill.

She panted as she slowly made her way up the weed-riddled sidewalk, her breath growing more labored as she ascended. The flats of Frontier View had not prepared her for the precipitous elevations of Duluth. Though her legs and lungs complained bitterly, she pressed on, unwilling to risk losing sight of her brother.

At the crest of the hill, she rested her hands on her thighs, stopping to catch her breath. She spied her brother just as he made a sharp left turn, disappearing from her sight. Shaking off her weariness, Emiko hurried on.

Around the corner loomed a large, concrete school building, surrounded by a wide expanse of waist-tall grass. Nathan brushed through the grass, toward the school.

Where is he going? Emiko trailed him through the grass, creeping ahead with her back hunched and her knees bent, concealing herself and the rifle on her back as best she could. As her hands swept the grass aside, plumes of pollen swirled behind her.

A sudden jolt of pain pulsed through her foot as she badly stubbed her toe and stumbled forward. After regaining her balance, she looked down at what she'd kicked — a flat, roughly polished, rectangular stone, engraved with the words:

IN MEMORY OF S. O'OONNOR
1998 - 2027

So, they used this schoolyard as a cemetery. Standing tall and looking around, she realized that wood and stone tombstones, many partially hidden by the grass, surrounded her on all sides.

She was treading on the bodies of the dead.

The open field must have been a convenient burial site after the Desolation virus swept through Duluth. But what was Nathan doing here? Emiko ducked down into the grass again and, risking discovery, she moved quickly to get closer to him.

A short distance ahead, Nathan stopped abruptly. He stared at the ground momentarily, before suddenly kneeling and disappearing into the foliage. Emiko could see only his black hair, protruding from the grass.

Nathan remained on his knees for several minutes. *What could he possibly be doing in such a creepy place?* The hot sun of late afternoon bore down as Emiko waited for his next move. The open schoolyard offered no shadows under which to hide.

Finally, Nathan rose, and began heading back in Emiko's direction. Emiko hastily fell to the ground, lying on her belly. Her heart beat wildly against the soft earth. If Nathan saw her here, what would happen? Would he be angry? Would he send her back to Frontier View? Would Pierre take away her new rifle? What would Beard think?

She squeezed her eyes shut. Maybe if she couldn't see her brother, he'd be unable to see her.

The grass rustled. In her mind, she pictured her brother walking directly toward her, his blue jeans rubbing against the tall grass.

The rustling suddenly stopped. Nathan was no longer moving.

Emiko held her breath. Had he seen her? She dug her fingernails into the dirt, clinging fast to the ground as though she were a swimmer lost at sea, clutching a piece of driftwood.

She heard her brother emit a deep sigh and wipe away a sniffle, before resuming his walk across the field. Eventually, the rustling of his pants against the grass faded into the distance.

Emiko remained prone, listening to the wind whistle across the wild prairie. Certain that Nathan had left, she slowly gathered herself and trotted to the place where he'd stood.

At her feet was a simple tombstone, resting flat against the earth. It read:

RYOTA KANNO
LOVING FATHER. DEVOTED HUSBAND. DESOLATION SURVIVOR.
1985 - 2035
MAY HIS SOUL REST IN PEACE

Emiko's gaze froze on the inscription. Her lower lip quivered. Like a shotgun kick to her heart, she now fully understood what Nathan had felt the year before. He'd come to Duluth together with their father only to leave forever without him.

Chapter 10

LATER THAT NIGHT, long after the sun had set on Duluth, John ventured out along the brick-paved streets of the city center. His shadow alternatively grew and shrunk as it passed through the amber glow of the kerosene lamps. To his surprise, the street also sported a handful of electric lights. Though electricity was scarce, a few bars and restaurants had scavenged the materials necessary to generate power. Flickering neon signs created a gaudy splash of color, the most resplendent sight John had seen since before the Desolation.

A sign, posted in front of an establishment called The Drunken Loon, caught John's eye. The bar's name glowed in red. Above it hung the outline of a loon in vibrant blue and white neon. Heavy rock music pulsated from inside.

Proceeding toward the door, John noticed a car parked behind a wagon on the side of the street. Putting his desire for a drink on hold temporarily, he strode closer. The car was an old, black Japanese sedan — the Honda Civic that had passed him and Nathan on the highway to Duluth.

John circled the car, curious about who owned it and how they obtained fuel for it. Tinted windows prevented him from seeing inside, and the car's exterior offered no clues. It had no license plates, and all of its identifying marks, including the Honda logos, had been stripped.

His curiosity unsatisfied, John returned to The Drunken Loon. The bar was housed in the first floor of an old red brick hotel, a relic from the age of jazz and prohibition. Looking through its large rectangular windows, John saw more electric lights and a lively crowd drinking and dancing.

He pushed the door inward, allowing the pounding rock music to escape into the night air. Though the song, a vicious mixture of distorted guitars and machine gun drums, sounded familiar, he couldn't place it. The chorus blared, with the singer shrieking "Death, bodies, blood, bath!" over the heavy, crunching guitar riffs.

The bar's interior was expansive. On the left was a counter manned by two bartenders. To the right was ample standing room flanked by a smattering of chairs and tables. The wooden decor was well-used but clean. It was clear that the bar's managers made a point of keeping the place in good order — an unwritten law of humanity dictated that the finer things in life required more upkeep than the essentials. Establishing an oasis of paradise in the north was no easy task, especially given the manpower required to make the most of a short growing season.

A smoky haze enveloped the bar's interior. John picked out the distinct scent of tobacco mingled with other, less familiar odors. Shuffling through the crowd, he pried himself into an opening between two other patrons and rested his elbows on the counter. A moment later, a bartender approached.

"What can I get you?" the bartender shouted over the music.

"A tall mug of beer."

"You want the Superior Stout or the Loony Lager?" The bartender pointed to a pair of taps. One was topped by a carved loon head, the other with a carved fish.

John couldn't remember the last time he'd been offered a choice of beers. The usual options were to either drink moose piss or stay dry.

"The stout," John said, scratching his chin with his thumb.

With a nod, the bartender held a glass mug under the tap. Pure, brown beer slowly filled the mug. When the bartender finished, only a thin layer of foam graced the top. He slid the mug across the counter to John.

"Two dollars," he said.

John produced a blue Minnesota fiver from his pocket — all the cash he had on hand — and gave it to the bartender, who put it in the cash register and returned to hand him three singles in change. John left one on the counter and pocketed the other two before turning his attention back to room behind him.

One corner was occupied by a group of men sporting plaid shirts and jeans — likely a party of hunters, loggers, or other woodsy tradesmen. In another corner a fashionable young man and a tantalizingly curvaceous woman shared a table. The man wore a sharp black polo shirt. His hair was slicked back and greasy. The woman wore a flowery blue sorority sister dress and high heels. She was clearly unenthused by their conversation. In the center of the bar a few young adults — kids who wouldn't have been of legal drinking age, had such requirements still existed — danced wildly to the heavy music. They flailed their arms, bobbed their heads, and let their long hair swing freely. The colorful variety of clientele lent the bar an interesting atmosphere. Before the Desolation, each group would've had a watering hole that catered to its unique tastes. Now, everyone drank together in one place.

After scanning the crowd, John made his way to a doorway along the back wall. There he spotted a couple of pool tables, their playing surfaces covered with smooth green felt. Near the tables were two men, taking turns tossing darts at a fully functional electronic dartboard in the rear corner of the room. One had bushy eyebrows and wide, powerful shoulders. The other was tall and thin with a toothy grin. Both carried pistols on their hips and wore green vests — the same green vests John had encountered while rescuing Nathan's sister from Sawbill Lake.

Recalling Sawbill Lake, John bristled. He reached across his body to give his left bicep a gentle squeeze. Did they have anything to do with Emiko's kidnapping? More importantly, did they know anything about his arm?

The hotel clerk had mentioned that John and Nathan's neighbors were two men with a car who liked to play darts. Had she been speaking of these two? If so, it could make for an awkward night. John took a long, contemplative sip of his beer, before setting the mug down and approaching the men.

"You boys mind if I join you?" John asked the broad, burly man.

"Fine by me. What do you say, Leonard?" the burly man asked his partner.

The tall man shrugged, flashing his toothy smile. "Sure, why not?"

"Sounds like we have ourselves a game. I'm Smitty," the burly man said as he took his place at the throwing line. "And this is my partner, Leonard." He nodded at his beanpole of an accomplice.

"The name's John. John Osborne."

Leonard narrowed his eyes and stared at John. John returned his gaze, unblinking.

Leonard rubbed his chin. "Have we met before?"

"Hard to say," John answered. "Small world." If they'd met previously, John couldn't say where or when.

Leonard cocked his head and furrowed his brow, continuing to size John up. With a grimace, he turned away and snatched the plastic darts from Smitty.

"We're almost finished with this game," Smitty said. "Give us a moment."

The scoreboard read 45 - 201 in Smitty's favor. John suspected the two men were playing 501. If he recalled correctly, the objective was to be the first to reach zero without going under.

After Leonard completed his turn, Smitty stepped to the line. He hit a double 19 followed by a single 7 for a total of 45 points, ending the game. The machine's display flashed frenetically and played a short celebratory melody.

"What do you say we make things interesting?" Smitty grinned, showing two rows of teeth, slightly yellowed but straight. "Each man bets ten bucks. Winner takes all. Leonard?"

"I'm in."

"John?"

"Why not?" John said, undeterred by the fact that he didn't have ten dollars to lose. Lady luck favored the skillful and bold.

"Great. Leonard, fire up the board. 501 for three."

Leonard pressed a couple of buttons. The machine's display played a short video clip of a dart hitting a bullseye, and the game began.

"Newcomers first," Smitty said, offering the darts to John.

John wet his lips and stepped forward. He threw with his naturally dominant hand, his right. His first dart hit the board just outside the circle — a miss. His second dart hit a single three, and his third dart a double six, lowering his score from 501 to 486.

"A bit rusty, eh?" Smitty said. "Leonard, go ahead."

John frowned, handing the darts to Leonard. Three throws later, Leonard ended his turn with 475 points.

Smitty threw next, hitting a triple 20 on his way to a cool 422.

"Is that your car out there?" John asked casually as he took the darts from Smitty.

"Why would you think that?" Smitty replied.

"Two strapping young men such as yourselves seem just the types with enough know-how to get a car up and running."

John continued to throw as he chatted. His second round went only slightly better than his first.

Smitty's lips curved into a half-smirk. "I can't turn down a compliment like that. Yeah, it's our car. What of it?"

"Mind if I ask where you got the fuel?"

Smitty eyed Leonard, silently requesting his input on the matter. Leonard shrugged indifferently as he toed the line.

"Some guys we know have an oil refinery up and running in central Canada," Leonard said. "We got the gas there. Car, too."

"Central Canada? That's a long way to travel just to pick up a car with a full tank of gas."

"Sure is."

"We have our reasons," Smitty said, taking the darts from Leonard.

"That so?" John said.

Smitty didn't offer a response. He threw, lowering his score to 357, then passed the darts to John.

John stared at the darts in his palm. If that's all these two men would offer up about their car, John didn't imagine they'd have much to say about their employer, either ... at least not without a little coercion. For the time being, John decided not to press the issue. He continued to play, limiting his chatter to small talk about the game at hand.

Darts sped through the air one by one, each hitting the board with a dull thud. Smitty kept throwing well, while Leonard struggled. In the end, Smitty won the game handily, hitting zero with John languishing at 152 and Leonard trailing far behind at 229.

"Looks like you boys owe me ten apiece."

John watched Leonard fish through his pockets, digging for cash. He then turned to Smitty, staring straight into the burly man's eyes.

"Double or nothing," he said.

Smitty chuckled. "Double or nothing, eh? You sure? Seems to me you'll just get your ass handed to you again."

John drew his eyebrows together, narrowing his eyes. "I'm sure."

"It's your funeral, my friend," Smitty said. His smile widened, putting his incisors on display.

"Ten is enough for me. I'm out." Leonard held up his palms in surrender. "I'm gonna get myself another drink." He slapped a blue Minnesota ten-spot on the pool table nearest the dart board and retreated into the bar's main room.

"Just you and me," John said.

"Guess so," Smitty replied. "Loser first?"

"Why not?" John grunted, stepping to the board and yanking the darts free. "Someone must be paying you well if you have twenty bucks to blow on a game of darts."

"Judging from the results of our first match, I don't think I have much to worry about," Smitty shot back.

"Just the same, I'd like to know who you work for. I've been looking for work myself."

"Want my advice? If I were in your boots, the first thing I'd do is shave off that muskrat you got hanging from your chin."

John glowered at Smitty. "I'll take it under consideration."

"I'm sure my boss could find a few other reasons to disqualify you, as well."

John tilted his head back slightly, sticking out his bearded chin. He then took a dart, this time in his left hand. With a flick of his wrist and only the slightest motion of his elbow, he directed it at the board. He nailed a triple 20, netting 60 points, the maximum possible from a single dart.

"Decided to make it a game this time, eh?" Smitty said.

John didn't dignify the comment with a reply. Immediately, he took his next dart and repeated the feat, netting 60 more. His last dart produced the same result, a third consecutive triple 20.

He'd hit a perfect round of 180 points — dart enthusiasts called it a ton 80 — which left his score at 321. He walked up to the board, curled his fingers around the three darts, and yanked them free.

Smitty accepted the darts without comment.

"What would your boss think of that?" John asked, picking up his beer mug and taking a deep sip.

In lieu of speaking, Smitty instead responded by taking his turn. He notched his best round of the day, scoring 121 points between the three darts, but it paled in comparison to John's perfect 180 point display of skill. After admiring his handiwork, he fetched the darts and passed them to John.

"All downhill for you from here," Smitty grunted.

"Don't bet on it," John retorted, stepping to the line. He fired all three darts in rapid succession, quickly transferring them from his right palm to the grip of his left thumb and forefinger.

The machine flashed inanely and rang out with a cheerful ditty, congratulating John for scoring another ton 80. His score stood at 141. He plucked the darts from the board and held them out for Smitty, who took them without a word.

Smitty racked up 98 points with his next three throws — enough to lower his score to 282, impressive under ordinary circumstances. After yanking his darts from the board, he glared and shoved the darts against John's chest.

"Here," he muttered.

John collected the feathered projectiles and once again stepped to the line.

"Triple 17," he said, calling his shot. His dart whooshed straight and true through the haze of the bar, and the scoreboard read 90.

"Double 20," he announced. The second dart whistled through the air like a crossbow bolt, hit its mark, and dropped his score to 50.

"Bullseye," he calmly proclaimed. However, as he was about to release his final dart, he felt a hand tightly clasp his wrist. The dart slipped from John's fingers, clattering on the ground as it fell far short of the dart machine.

"That's enough," Smitty scowled. "I saw you change hands. What's the deal? You a frickin' hustler?"

"I dunno, pal." John wrenched his arm free of the man's grip. "Answer this: are you a frickin' kidnapper?"

Smitty's expression contorted into a mix of contempt and confusion. "I got no idea what you're talking about." He retreated a step and rested his palms on the rail of the nearby pool table.

"Four of your kind," John seethed, grabbing Smitty's vest by the collar. "Four men wearing these silly green uniforms kidnapped a good friend of mine a few weeks back. You're telling me you don't know anything about that?"

A bead of sweat rolled down Smitty's forehead. "I don't know anything about a kidnapping."

"Maybe that's true," John said, tightening his grip on the man's collar. "But even if you're as clueless as you claim, I think whoever you work for knows something. I want his name."

"You're not gonna get it from of me." Smitty spit, producing a juicy glob of saliva that landed at John's feet.

John slammed his right fist into Smitty's gut. Smitty groaned, struggling against the reflexive urge to double over.

"You sure?" John said.

"Sure as I'm gonna stick a rack of whitetail antlers up your ass," Smitty sputtered, raising both hands from the rail and clutching John's shoulders. He threw his head forward, swinging it at John's temple like a lumberjack's axe.

John leaned to one side, easily dodging the headbutt. He thrust his left arm up, breaking Smitty's shoulder hold, then wrapped both hands around the man's neck.

"That, my friend, was a mistake," he said, lifting Smitty so that the burly man's toes just barely kissed the ground. "I asked you who you work for." John stared icily into Smitty's panicked eyes. "When you're ready to talk, I'm ready to listen."

Smitty's struggled helplessly against John's grip. The veins in his neck bulged under John's fingers. The seconds ticked by. Smitty gave no sign he was ready to give in.

"Put him down," a voice called out. "Or else."

John's eyes darted toward the voice. The other man, Leonard, stood in the doorway. His shaky hands gripped a dull silver semi-automatic pistol, leveled at John's head.

John smelled fear emanating from the tall, skinny man. Unfortunately, the man's fear wouldn't alter the course of a .45 round at fifteen feet.

"Tell me who you work for and I let him go," John said assertively, despite knowing he'd lost his advantage.

"You let him go or I shoot you dead." Leonard looked ready to piss his pants, his body language belying his words.

"Suit yourself."

Tapping into the super-human strength of his left arm, John heaved Smitty into the air, flinging him like a rag doll. Smitty flew toward the doorway, where Leonard stood petrified in wide-eyed amazement. Smitty collided with Leonard, hitting him like a bowling ball crashing into a pin. Even from a distance, John could feel the air rushing out of both their lungs.

Suddenly, John felt woozy. He teetered back and forth, trying to maintain his balance. Pain rippled through his stomach, causing him to double over.

Why is my body betraying me? I barely tapped into the arm's power.

John shook his head violently. He had to focus. The two men wouldn't be stunned for long.

He stumbled over the bodies of the two men as he passed through the door into the main room. The thundering rock music throbbed in his ears. His breathing became labored. Soon he found himself tripping over his own feet, narrowly breaking his fall by planting his right hand on the grimy floor.

"Hey man, what's your problem?" a deep voice said, barely audible over the loud music.

John felt vomit rushing up his throat. He opened his mouth and spewed an acrid mix of bile and alcohol onto the floor.

"Christ, how much did that guy drink?" another voice shouted.

Someone grabbed John's arm. "You gonna be alright?" they asked.

"I'll … be … fine," John coughed out, struggling to find space for the words between gulps of air. Rising to his feet, he jerked his arm free of the stranger's grip and continued to stagger through the crowd toward the bar's exit.

Chapter 11

AT DUSK NATHAN returned to the Lakefront Inn. He found the hotel room unoccupied, suggesting John had already gone out for the evening. After pacing back and forth across the carpeted floor for a time, Nathan turned his attention to tidying up the spartan room. He fluffed the pillows and straightened the sheets, just as he did every morning in Frontier View. The familiar routine of cleaning up after his sister helped settle his thoughts.

Would his father be proud of what he'd accomplished over the past year? What would he think of Nathan's cross-Minnesota journey with the mysterious vagabond, John Osborne? Would he scold Nathan for leaving his sister behind? Visiting his father's grave had provided no answers.

Housekeeping completed, Nathan checked to see that the tvapa was fed and watered. He then left the inn and made his way through the streets of downtown Duluth. The muted radiance of the street lamps and the shimmering reds, greens, and blues of the neon signs lit his way. By now, John was likely cradling a beer and was discovering firsthand what a drunken loon looked like.

Nathan still often wondered why John had agreed to bring him along. He could hunt, but he was no marksman; he willingly performed physical work, but it would be a stretch to call him strong. Though he thought himself bright, as of yet there'd been no use for the muscle that lay between his ears. Perhaps John merely wanted to give an eager young soul a chance to see the world?

No, Nathan thought, *that wouldn't be very John-like*. Though he didn't understand the bearded man's inner workings, Nathan knew John's every action was driven by purpose.

Nathan followed the directions the hotel clerk had given. Just as she'd promised, The Drunken Loon was impossible to miss. A vibrant, cheery neon sign invited guests inside, and already there was a man lying in a drunken stupor on the sidewalk out front. As Nathan drew nearer, he realized that the man wasn't just another drunken lout.

"John!" Nathan dashed to his partner, kneeling at his side. John was lying face down, unconscious but still breathing.

"John, are you alright?" Nathan felt John's neck for a pulse. His heart was beating strong and fast, as though he were exerting himself physically. Nathan's thoughts raced back to when Emiko had first discovered John outside of Frontier View. Remembering how that situation had played out, Nathan had a bad feeling John wouldn't wake up any time soon.

What did you get yourself into this time, John? He saw no choice but to drag John's limp body back to their hotel, where he could monitor the unconscious man's condition. If there was no change by morning, he'd bring John to the hospital … the hospital where his dad had died. Nathan heaved an anxious breath, pursing his lips. He had to focus on the present.

As he gripped John beneath the shoulders, two men burst through the door of The Drunken Loon. Both men had pistols, drawn and ready.

"Where did that moose turd lickin' bastard go?"

"He couldn't have gotten far. He'll be easy to find with that beard of his."

The two men looked straight at Nathan, who was just beginning to move John's unconscious body.

"There he is!" the burlier of the two called out. He aimed his pistol at Nathan.

Loons over the moon! The muscles in Nathan's neck grew taut. His hair stood on end. Taking another look at the men, he realized they wore identical familiar-looking green vests.

"Who the Desolation are you guys?" he blurted out.

"We're gonna be your worst nightmare, if you don't get your ass out of here right now," said the skinnier man.

"I can't do that," Nathan stammered, doing his best to steady his quivering voice.

"Look, kid," the burly man said. "Maybe you know this guy, maybe you don't. I don't know and I don't care. If you leave now, we'll let you go, no questions asked."

Nathan had no weapon. Even if he'd had his Remington, he'd never stand a chance against two angry, hot-headed men with guns already drawn. Still, John was his partner, and the men's attire suggested a connection to Emiko's kidnapping.

"No," Nathan countered, resolutely. "Wherever you take him, you're taking me, too."

"Or we put a bullet through your brain, throw your body in Lake Superior, and take your friend anyway," the skinny man said.

"Laying it on a little thick, aren't you, Leonard?" the burly man grumbled. "This little Chinese whelp can't be older than thirteen."

"Japanese. Half-Japanese," Nathan protested. "And I'm sevent —"

"Shut the hell up," Leonard waved his pistol at Nathan. "Come on, Smitty, let's just knock him out and take the bearded guy."

Smitty nodded, and the two men inched toward Nathan, moving forward with care despite clearly having the upper hand. Nathan took a deep, bracing breath and held his position.

Gunfire shattered the still night air. Nathan winced reflexively, nearly dropping John. As the sound echoed through the streets, Nathan realized he hadn't been hit.

"Moose on the loose! Where did that come from?" Leonard cried out, retreating toward The Drunken Loon.

"From somewhere down the road," Smitty yelled, leaning his back against the bar's exterior wall. "I saw a muzzle flash over that way." He tilted his head to indicate the location.

Nathan didn't know who'd fired the shot, nor did he care. He hastily tightened his grip on John and began dragging him toward the far side of the street.

"Hey — don't move!" Leonard called out.

Nathan stood still, struggling to support John's body in his arms. His great escape had lasted all of a second and half.

Leonard centered Nathan in his sights of his pistol. "Try that crap again and you're a dead man."

Another shot rang out. Leonard's pistol flew from his hand.

"Yeouccch!" he cried, shaking his arm. He hadn't been hit directly, but the force of the dislodging pistol had likely left him with jammed fingers.

Smitty glowered at Nathan. He still had his pistol in hand, its muzzle pointed at the sidewalk. Swifter than a jittery gopher, he swung his arms up and aimed the gun at Nathan. Just as quickly, the mystery rifleman fired again. The pistol was torn from Smitty's grasp.

"Desolation!" Smitty roared with rage. He turned, shouting into the darkness, "Whoever the hell you are, we're coming to get you!" After retrieving his pistol, which now had a sizeable dent in its barrel, he dashed to the driver's side of the black car and hopped in.

"Wait for me!" Leonard cried, picking up his pistol and tearing after Smitty. As Leonard plopped into the passenger seat, the car roared to life. The tires squealed and the black vehicle tore off.

Nathan seized the opportunity to tug John into the nearby alley. His heart pumped with such force he feared his veins would burst.

In the alley, he managed to rest John's limp body against a dumpster. The fetid odor of rancid meat fouled the air. Though he hoped the horrible stench would rouse his partner, he expected no such good fortune. After ensuring John's body wasn't readily visible, Nathan sprinted for the hotel.

Who was the unknown shooter who had saved him? Nathan hadn't the slightest clue. He had no acquaintances in Duluth. Could it have been friend of John's? No, John didn't know anyone here, either. As the Lakefront Inn came into view, the best guess Nathan had was that it'd been a member of a vigilante peace-keeping organization — a guardian angel.

The sight of his hotel room door gave Nathan pause. *The clerk said our neighbors had a car*, he recalled. How could he have forgotten? Returning to the hotel had been foolish. The two men could arrive at any time. Still, he was already here. He couldn't leave empty handed.

He burst into the room. In a frenzy he stuffed their belongings into their two backpacks. He threw one pack onto his back and the other across his chest. Then, tossing the room key on his bed, he dashed out the door and carried the double-load of gear up to the stable.

Nathan charged inside to find Mumford still awake, standing idly beside the cart. Nathan arranged the two packs inside of the canoe, which sat upright atop the cart. He hitched the cart to Mumford and jerked the reins to direct the tvapa onto the street.

While trying to appear inconspicuous, Nathan glanced back and forth, desperately hoping the two men wouldn't return. His pulse throbbed audibly in his ears; the city lights flared with each beat of his heart.

They soon were back in the alley. John hadn't moved.

"Alright, in you go," Nathan commanded, trying to hoist John arms first into the canoe. With difficulty, he managed to get John's arms to hang over the gunwale, but when he tried to lift his legs, John's limp arms slid out from the canoe and his body slammed to the ground.

Nathan grimaced as though he had also experienced the blow. Changing his tack, he lifted John's legs into the canoe. Then, with the manliest grunt he could muster, he heaved John's upper body into the aluminum craft.

Wiping his hands clean, Nathan examined the load. Two packs and an unconscious man sat in the middle of the metal hull, positioned so that the canoe would maintain its balance on the short wooden cart.

There was no time to dally. Nathan led the tvapa through the streets of Duluth, listening intently for the roar of a car engine. The roar never came, and within the hour Nathan and his comatose partner had escaped Duluth. Heading north under the cover of moonlight, they resumed the long journey toward International Falls, Rainy Lake, and Mallard Island. A barred owl hooted plaintively. Wolves howled in the distance.

Chapter 12

EMIKO LAY FLAT on her belly, hiding underneath a booth seat inside a deserted breakfast diner. The restaurant smelled of mold and cat feces, and a thick layer of dust caked the floor. Unlike many other buildings in downtown Duluth, this one had seen no post-Desolation renovations.

Emiko tried to breathe quietly as she listened for a passing car outside. Beside her rested the Springfield rifle, its magazine empty. When the two men threatened her brother and Beard — who looked like he was in bad shape — she'd done all she could to help, giving no consideration to how the men would react. That the two assailants wore the same green uniforms her kidnappers had worn had only heightened her fury.

Those justifications, however, wouldn't change the fact that she'd acted rashly, nor that the men's pursuit had caught her off guard. Now she was in trouble.

The dust in the air tickled Emiko's nose. She did her best to stifle the sneeze that followed. Despite her efforts, the rush of air from her nose caused a storm of dust to rise from the floor.

Outside she heard the approaching car. Its engine grew louder, drawing closer. The sound dropped to a low hum before cutting out completely. Two car doors opened and slammed shut in quick succession, followed by the patter of footsteps.

Why didn't I run when I had the chance? Emiko silently griped, nervously biting at her lower lip. It was too late to escape now. She reached into her pocket. Inside were her last two .30-06 rounds. She was confident that she could load them quickly. Could she do so without being heard or seen? That was less certain. Hopefully the two men would leave before she had to find out.

"Leonard, take a look at this," a man's voice trickled in from the street through a broken window. "It's a shell casing."

Emiko cringed, her muscles tightening. She'd been lying prone on the sidewalk when she'd fired. Though she'd had no cover, the darkness of night had concealed her well enough. Only the muzzle flashes had betrayed her position.

"Looks like a .30-06 cartridge," the other man, Leonard, said. "Doesn't tell us much about our shooter."

"No, it doesn't. But he's one hell of a good shot," the first man replied. "I'd like to know what kind of gear he's using."

He? Emiko clenched her fist tightly. Did men always assume that only other men knew how to shoot?

"We'd best be careful," the first man continued. "It'll be safer if we split up. You go inside. I'll cover the exterior. If you hear gunfire, find a way around the back of the building and see if you can get better position on our shooter. I'll do the same."

"Why don't you go inside, Smitty?" Leonard complained.

"Just do it, Leonard," Smitty growled. "It's safer in there. A good sniper wouldn't let us trap him in a corner."

Emiko frowned. They had her profile all wrong. Maybe they wouldn't even recognize her as the sniper. *Maybe, if I didn't have this rifle in my hands.*

The diner's door swung open. One of the men entered. Shards of glass crunched beneath his boots. He paced around the room, his legs passing in and out of Emiko's limited range of sight.

Taking care to remain silent, Emiko fished a live round from her pocket. She wanted a bullet in her palm, ready to be fed into the Springfield's magazine.

The intruder neared Emiko's hiding spot. Her palpitating heart reminded her that she was not well hidden. At the proper angle, the man wouldn't even need to crouch to see her.

The man stopped, his boots inches from Emiko's eyes. If he bent over to look beneath the bench, she was as good as gone.

Her nostril's tingled. Another sneeze was coming. If she moved to pinch her nose, she'd risk being discovered. *Better to hold it in as best I can*, she thought.

The man shifted his feet. One boot remained flat on the floor, while the heel of the other pulled away. He was crouching. Struggling to hold her sneeze, Emiko drew the live round in her hand closer to her rifle. She'd have to load quickly to have a chance — faster than even Beard could load a rifle.

Somewhere outside, a dog barked. The first bark was promptly followed by more barks and yelps, reverberating through the warm night air.

"Leonard, you find anything?" a voice shouted from outside.

"Nothing." The man in front of Emiko stopped mid-crouch, his knee suspended just above the dining booth seat. "You?"

"Same. I don't think our man is here. I say we go see what these dogs are so upset about."

"Alright, I'm coming." The man stood and headed for the door. As he walked out, Emiko moved to pinch her nose, her clothing rustling against the grime-covered floor.

Out front, the car engine turned over. The engine growled louder as the vehicle accelerated, before fading into the distance.

At last, Emiko released her sneeze, letting it escape her nose in a furious rush. She waited a few minutes to make sure the men wouldn't return, then walked out of the diner, unsure of where to go. Eventually, she decided on the Lakefront Inn. She wasn't ready to reveal her presence to Nathan, not even after her heroics, but she did want to confirm that he and Beard were safe.

As she walked, Emiko mulled over her next step. She could remain hidden, continuing to trail her brother and Beard to Mallard Island. Her other option was to expose herself and face the consequences, in hopes that the two men would be grateful she'd saved them and therefore agree to let her accompany them. She weighed the choices in her head.

Reaching the hotel didn't take long. Her brother's room was dark and the door was cracked open. She crept closer to take a peek inside. Worst case scenario? If Nathan saw her, she could dart away.

It turned out there was no need. Nathan's room was empty. The room key lay on the bed. Emiko went to check the stable. The cart and Mumford were also gone.

Nathan and Beard had disappeared into the night. Emiko was proud that her sharpshooting had enabled their escape.

Unfortunately, now that they were gone, she'd lost her best to opportunity explain the situation and join them. She could easily catch up — Mumford moved about as quickly as a hibernating bear. By tomorrow, however, once the heat of the moment had passed, Nathan would likely focus on her decision to leave Frontier View without permission rather than on tonight's brave act. She nervously circled the hotel's parking lot, unsure if she wanted to face her brother's wrath. If she didn't follow Nathan and Beard, what else could she do?

Emiko froze. In the distance, she heard a car. Were the green-vested men coming back for her? She bolted for Nathan and Beard's hotel room, entering and slamming the door shut. Leaning against the door, she rested the Springfield rifle across her thighs.

Did they know Nathan and Beard were staying here? she wondered. She clamped her eyes shut, but the growling of the car only grew louder. Eventually, the sound was right outside her door. The engine went silent. Two car doors opened and slammed shut.

How had they found her? She tightened her grip on the rifle.

"Smitty, you think they orchestrated all of this? The bar fight, the sniper, and the escape?"

"I dunno. That bearded guy was definitely eager to grill me for information, but he didn't do himself any favors by passing out in front of the bar. Maybe the sharpshooter in the shadows was their backup. Regardless, whatever their plan was, it didn't work."

Emiko gulped as two shadows passed by her window.

"You didn't say nothing, right?"

"I said their plan didn't work, Leonard," Smitty said, defensively. "That means that I didn't talk."

"Take it easy! I was just making sure."

Emiko heard one of the men fumbling with keys. *Why would they have keys to my room?* The clinking of the keys seemed strangely muted.

A door creaked open on its latches — not her door, but the door to the next room over.

She had neighbors. On hands and knees, she crawled to put her ear against the wall.

"Let's get some sleep," Smitty said. "We can find the guy tomorrow."

"With the car, it shouldn't be much trouble," Leonard said.

"I don't think we should use the car."

"Why?"

"We need the gas to get back to HQ."

"Good point. Makes our job harder, but we'll still find them."

"We can think about it in the morning. I'm ready to nod off right where I stand." Bedsprings squealed. "Good night."

"Night."

After a few minutes of silence, Emiko again heard bedsprings squeak, then nothing.

Taking care not to arouse her own bedsprings, Emiko gently climbed into bed and snuggled beneath the sheets. Lying in bed, she let the night's events sink in.

Her neighbors had assaulted Nathan and Beard. Their green vests suggested a connection with the men that had kidnapped her. Who were these men? What did they want with Beard, Nathan, and herself? Thinking about it made her blood boil.

As she drifted to sleep, Emiko contemplated what she should do next. Beard and Nathan had set out on their quest without her. Surely they could complete it without her, as well.

She had a mission of her own now. Her neighbors, Smitty and Leonard, had messed with the wrong girl.

* * *

The next morning Emiko awoke at dawn. Her first task was to rescale the lakeside building where she'd left her things the day before. She braved the rickety ladder, retrieved her pack, and returned to the hotel room. After carefully placing the

Springfield rifle underneath her bed and pulling the blankets closer to the floor to hide it, she made her way to the hotel's front office. The clang of a metal bell against the door undermined her intentions to enter quietly.

There was no one at the front desk. Emiko heard two muffled, female voices coming from behind a curtained doorway. Looking around the room, her attention was drawn to a large poster on the wall. Emiko didn't have any idea what "Aloha" meant, or why she'd want to say it, but the beach in the poster sure looked inviting. Northern Minnesota wasn't known for its beaches.

"Can I help you?" A woman swept the curtain aside and stepped toward Emiko. She had brunette hair, long albeit not as long as Emiko's. Though her youthful face looked tired, she still managed a bright smile.

Emiko stood tall with her arms at her sides. She looked the woman in the eye.

"Yes. I'm looking for work," she said.

"You're looking for work? Shouldn't you be in school?"

"School? Kids here go to school?" Emiko had heard about school from her brother but had never attended one herself. That said, even in Frontier View her father had always made sure she spent at least a few hours a day studying, with a focus on math and science. Recently, however, she'd often forgone her studies to spend more time hunting.

"Generally speaking, yes, they do." The woman nodded. "I take it you're not from around here?" She paused, examining Emiko closely. "Come to think of it, you look an awful lot like that cute, geeky guy who booked a room here yesterday. Your brother, by chance?"

Emiko hesitated before answering. "Yes. He and Beard — I mean, my friend John — stayed here last night, but they had to leave early on some business. They told me that I should stay here a few more days and wait for them, but my fool of a brother forgot to leave money to pay for a room. So, I want to work for a room, and maybe some food." She nodded firmly as she finished her explanation, trying her best to appear strong and independent. From her dealings with Nathan and the other villagers in Frontier View, she'd come to understand that how she presented herself was just as important as the words she chose.

The woman's pupils shifted up and down as she sized up Emiko.

"What's your name?"

"Emiko."

"And where are you from, Emiko?"

"Frontier View."

"Never heard of it. Up north?"

"Yeah. It's a small town, inside the Boundary Waters Canoe Area."

"Inside the BWCA? Sounds like a rough life." The woman laid one arm across the desk, resting her chin on her other hand.

"The winters are rough, but we do alright." Emiko offered a smile.

"Well, I'm sure you're an old hand when it comes to living in the woods, but this is a hotel. Do you know what's involved in running a hotel?"

"Of course," Emiko lied, giving a single nod.

"If we employed you here, do you know what your responsibilities would be?"

"Yes."

"Mmm-hmm." The woman raised her eyebrows, beckoning Emiko to continue.

"Well, I guess I'd have to sweep the floors, wash the windows, shake out the carpets, make the beds, and do the laundry," she said, listing off all the chores that her brother often asked her to do — a list of requests which she nearly always brushed off.

"That's the bulk of it. And do you have any idea how long it'll be before your brother comes back to get you?"

Emiko shrugged. "A few days, I think. He didn't say exactly."

"Alright then. Wait here while I talk to the owner for a moment." She pointed to the curtained-off area with her thumb.

"Of course," Emiko said. "Oh, and I'd like to keep my brother's room, if that's okay."

"We'll see. By the way, my name's Janice."

"It's a pleasure to meet you, Janice," Emiko said, watching her disappear into the back room. Janice began chatting with another woman, but the heavy curtain prevented Emiko from overhearing the conversation.

I think I made a good impression, Emiko thought. She didn't expect she'd like the hotel work much, as it was the same kind of work she'd spent her whole life avoiding. Back in Frontier View, Nathan could've glued a broom to her hands and she still would have refused to sweep their cabin floor. This, however, was a serious job, and she swore to herself that she'd give her best effort. Anything less would ruin her plans.

The door bell clanged against the door. Emiko felt her hair stand on end.

Relax, Emiko, she told herself. *Even if it's those men, they won't recognize you. They never saw you.*

Emiko spun on her heels, turning to greet the newcomers. Indeed, it was the two men from the night before. They were clad in the same green vests they'd worn the night before. This morning, however, they no longer had holstered pistols. Dark circles underneath their eyes suggested they hadn't slept well.

"Good morning," one said. From his voice, Emiko knew he was Smitty. He was tall and powerful, like a brown bear, with thick, dark eyebrows that complemented his heavy jaw.

That meant that the other man was Leonard. He had a slim build and big front teeth, a combination which lent him the appearance of an undernourished rodent. He crossed his long arms and gave Emiko a curious look.

"Say, have I seen you somewhere before?" he said.

"I don't believe so."

Leonard scratched his chin with a long, pencil-like finger.

"Do you have an older brother?"

"Yes, I do," Emiko said, perhaps too eagerly. She smiled and batted her eyelids. "Why?"

"Well, we had a little trouble with one of your kind last night, you see."

"With one of my kind, you say?"

"Yeah, some Asian kid. He your brother?"

"Mister, there are a lot of Asians here in Duluth. You think some guy is my brother just because we have the same skin color?"

"Well, when you put it that way, you know, that's not what I —"

Smitty frowned, elbowing Leonard in the ribs. "Drop it," he muttered with a shake of his head.

"Emiko," Janice's voice called out as she emerged from behind the curtain. Assessing the situation, she eyed Emiko. "Are you bothering the customers again?"

"Again?" Emiko blinked in surprise. Was Janice covering for her?

"She's not bothering us at all, miss," Smitty replied.

"Good to hear. She's a bit of a handful sometimes. Now, Emiko, why don't you go back to room 107? I'll join you in a minute and then we can get to work on the day's tasks."

"Sure thing!" Emiko said, nodding vigorously before heading toward the door.

"It looks like we're going to be in town for another day or two. Is our room still vacant tonight?" Leonard asked.

"Sure is, just for you two," Janice replied.

Emiko pushed her way out the glass door, cutting herself out of the conversation. Back in room 107, she sat down against the wall she shared with the two men and waited.

Her plan was unfolding as well as she could've hoped. Janice had granted her request, and the two men, despite their suspicions, didn't recognize her. Still, she would need to be careful around them. She'd keep them at a distance, just as she would a hulking bull moose.

The door of the adjacent room opened and slammed shut. Putting her ear against the wall, Emiko eavesdropped on her neighbors.

"Say, Smitty, I think I figured out why you thought that guy last night looked familiar."

"Oh yeah?"

"When you enlisted, did the General show you a photo?"

"A photo? Now that you mention it ..." Smitty paused. "And he told us to inform him if we ever saw the man, right?"

"Right," Leonard said. "I think it was that guy."

Emiko pushed her ear tighter to the wall, trying to catch every word. She was almost certain they were talking about Beard.

"He didn't have a beard in the photo," Smitty said.

"A man can grow a beard, you know. Not that anyone does anymore. The guy must have an independent streak."

That settled it — they were definitely talking about Beard.

"Okay, so we saw him. Now what? We can't exactly radio the General." Smitty's voice dripped with scorn.

"Are you still yammering on about the radio? Look, I was trying to fix it. How was I supposed to know that putting in a different battery would fry the whole thing?"

"Should've just let it be," Smitty said. Emiko imagined the man lifting a hand to his forehead.

"It wasn't working anyway!"

As the two men continued to argue about the radio, Emiko considered what she'd heard. She understood most everything, but a few pressing questions remained: Who was "the General" and why did he have a photo of Beard? These unknowns taunted her like key pieces missing a jigsaw puzzle. Unfortunately, she didn't imagine she'd find the pieces hidden between the cushions of the sofa like she always had in her youth.

A knock sounded on Emiko's door.

"Come in," she called out.

The door swung open. On the other side stood Janice.

"Are you ready to get to work?" she asked.

Emiko hopped to her feet.

"Ready as I'll ever be," Emiko said, suddenly feeling hesitant as visions of sweeping floors and cleaning carpets sprang to mind.

"Is that the attitude you're gonna bring to your first day of work?" Janice chided. "Come on, once we get started, we'll be done before you know it. Follow me."

Forcing a smile, Emiko followed Janice, stepping once again into the bright morning sun. She raised a hand to cover her eyes. Not a single cloud graced the sky.

"By the way, do you know those two men?"

Emiko shook her head. "I've never seen them before." The statement wasn't a lie, but it wasn't exactly the truth, either. Emiko decided not to worry about it.

"Strange. One of them was asking about you — about how long you'd worked here and the like."

"What'd you tell him?" Emiko asked, trying to mask her anxiety.

"I told them you'd been here for a while."

"A while can mean a lot of things."

"Exactly." Janice winked.

"Well, thank you," Emiko replied, unsure of what else to say.

"No problem. There's no honorable reason for grown men to be asking questions about a cute girl like you. Anyhow, first things first — let's go see how the animals are doing." Janice made her way to the incline that led to the hotel's stable. Emiko trailed close behind.

I wonder if this is what having an older sister feels like. The thought lingered in Emiko's mind as she commenced her first day of work.

Chapter 13

HIS HEAVY EYELIDS refused to open. His tired body had no intention of rising. Though John had never been one to sleep in, today he wanted nothing more than to rest in his cozy place of slumber and snooze the morning away.

As he lay quietly, listening to the chirping birds, he revisited the dreams he'd had the night before. A panoply of vivid images flashed across his closed eyelids, as though a movie projector were projecting scenes directly from his brain onto his own private cinema screen.

He was in a bar, in the shadowy backroom of the crowded establishment with two men. John invited them to play darts, promptly losing the first game in a display of inability so pathetic that it could only occur in the land of dreams. The rematch went well, however, until an argument broke out between John and his competitor, at which point —

"Ooof!" John grunted painfully. Opening his eyes, he was surprised to find he was lying inside an aluminum canoe, awkwardly positioned between two packs, with his arms hanging over the gunwales on either side. Directly ahead, Mumford's brown-and-white mottled flanks swayed to and fro. Alongside the tvapa walked Nathan, with a shotgun strapped across his back.

John's body bounced on the bottom of the canoe again — thanks to the potholed road, he now understood. He let out another grunt of discomfort. Ahead, Nathan looked over his shoulder, searching for the source of the noise.

"You're awake!" Nathan exclaimed as his eyes met John's. He slowed, dropping behind Mumford and coming up alongside John.

"I'm awake," John muttered. "How long was I out?"

Nathan counted on his fingers before replying, "Four nights. This is the fifth day since I found you unconscious."

"Unconscious?" The gears of John's memory churned as he tried to recall what had happened — the darts, the standoff, and his pain-wracked body stumbling through The Drunken Loon, toward the exit. The dream hadn't been a dream, after all.

"What happened to the two men?" John asked.

"The two men in the green vests?" Nathan asked. "Just as I found you, they burst from the door of the bar, weapons drawn. They didn't look happy."

"I beat them at darts."

"Must've been quite a game." Nathan looked at John quizzically, offering him a chance to reply.

John had nothing to say.

"You know," Nathan continued, "those men were wearing the same vests as the men who —"

"I know," John cut Nathan off. "I tried to get them talking, without much luck. I got the impression that they were grunts working for a larger organization. That said, they legitimately seemed to be in the dark about Emiko's kidnapping."

"So, we're still right where we started, on a blind march toward Mallard Island?"

"Yes and no. I didn't get any information, but now that we've seen the same group operating up north as well as in Duluth, we know they're casting a pretty wide net. Also, they were the ones driving that black car."

"I know. I saw them drive away in it."

"They just drove off?" John asked with a confused frown. "How did you manage to scare them away?" Even with his Remington shotgun in hand, John had trouble imagining Nathan emerging victorious from a standoff with the two armed men.

"I had help. Someone fired three shots from the darkness down the street to distract them. The second and third shots knocked the pistols from their hands, a stunt that would make even you jealous." Nathan grinned. "Maybe it was a friend of yours?"

"A friend?" John scoffed.

"Well, I certainly have no idea who it was. My best guess is that it was a member of the local Guardian Angels."

"Or perhaps someone else with a vendetta against those green-vested men."

Nathan rubbed his chin. "I hadn't thought of that."

"By the way, where are we?" John asked.

"I think we'll arrive in the City of Orr within a couple hours, though it's hard to say. There aren't many landmarks in this part of Minnesota."

John admired the towering white pines that bordered the road. The rough path they traveled was like a narrow river coursing through an endless plain, a slender brown thread leading them through the vast wilderness. As he continued to examine the greenery from the canoe, John's stomach let out a deep, desperate grumble.

"You must be hungry," Nathan said. "How about we stop for lunch."

"What's on the menu?"

"I took up the hunting duties in your stead. I bagged a whitetail a couple days ago. It was more meat than I could carry, but I took what I could and still have quite a bit left. Besides that, I've been eating gooseberries and wild parsnip roots I find along the road."

"Sounds good. I could use some protein."

Eager to get out of his cramped quarters, John gingerly stood in the canoe and hopped over its gunwale, landing on both feet. After an unsteady start he quickly matched the cart's pace. His jeans felt oddly loose, slowly riding down his hips. Perhaps he'd lost a few pounds while out cold? He tightened his belt a notch.

"How are you feeling?" Nathan said with obvious concern.

"Never better."

"You sure? I wanted to take you to a doctor, but I decided it was more important to get out of Duluth as fast as possible. I did my best to take care of you the same way as Cynthia did and hoped you'd wake up with time and rest."

John gazed down the road, to point where it curved behind a stand of birch. Though it was clear that the enhanced capabilities of his left arm put immense strain on his body, he was no closer to understanding the how and the why. He would have to avoid using the arm's strength until he had more answers.

"You made the right choice," he finally responded. "A doctor wouldn't have what I need. Let's hope Mallard Island does."

Chapter 14

EMIKO HUMMED TO herself as the rollers of her carpet sweeper gently clattered across the soft, fuzzy hotel room rug. Even though she thought the carpeting looked just as clean before sweeping as after, she persisted anyway, making sure to pass over every inch of carpet at least twice. She didn't want to disappoint Janice.

At the Lakefront Inn, every day was filled with chores: dusting the furniture and windowsills, changing the bedding, emptying the waste baskets, shaking the throw rugs, cleaning the windows, and tending the animals in the stable.

Though the job became easier with each passing day, Emiko wondered how much longer she'd have to keep at it. Ever since gleaning those precious few tidbits of information from Smitty and Leonard on her first day of work, she hadn't heard much. They were still staying in the adjacent hotel room, still searching for Beard and Nathan. Fortunately, despite their earlier suspicions, they didn't seem concerned about Emiko's presence next door.

The two men often grumbled about how the trail had gone cold, and Smitty occasionally gave Leonard a hard time about the broken radio. Their other conversations were usually about the nightlife in Duluth — the best they'd experienced in quite some time.

Emiko pushed and pulled the carpet sweeper, methodically moving about the room. With a final, graceful backpedaled step toward the door she declared the job finished. It was the last room — the last room on the first floor. Unfortunately, the carpets on the second floor still awaited her.

Janice had explained to Emiko that the mechanical carpet sweeper was a poor substitute for a powered vacuum cleaner, but that the scarcity of electricity left them with no choice. Emiko had never used a vacuum, but she could remember the roar of the one her mother had maneuvered across the floors of their home in Minneapolis. Had she known back then how much work it took to keep a house clean, Emiko imagined she would've been more helpful.

As she stepped out the door, she heard Janice calling for her.

"Emiko, could you come give me a hand? The carpets can wait — they aren't going anywhere."

Emiko rested the carpet sweeper against the wall and followed Janice, who was carrying a step ladder into the office. On the way there, she spotted Leonard crossing the parking lot, presumably returning to his room. Avoiding eye contact, Emiko hastily slipped into the front office.

"I want to replace the curtains." Janice pointed to a chair, where sky blue taffeta drapes were attached to a new white rod by a series of brass rings. "I'll climb the ladder. Your job is to hand the curtain rod up to me."

"Yes ma'am." Emiko smiled cordially. She wasn't sure if "ma'am" was entirely appropriate, but she didn't feel comfortable addressing her boss by her first name.

Janice made her way up the step ladder and called for the curtain rod, which Emiko promptly handed to her. The step ladder was short, leaving Emiko to wonder if Janice had really needed help.

"You know, Emiko, you haven't talked much about yourself," Janice said as she attempted to slot the rod onto two hooks that hung from the wall. "I met your brother. Was the bearded man with him your father?"

"John?" Emiko snorted. "No, he's just a friend of my brother's. My father passed away last year."

"I'm sorry to hear that. And what of your mother?"

"Taken by the Desolation."

"I lost my father during that time, as well," Janice said, as the curtain rod snapped into place. She adjusted the spacing of the rings, spreading the blue curtain evenly across the length of the rod. "It's hard to believe it's been almost a decade."

"Do you have any other family?" Emiko asked.

"I was an only child. My mom died about three years ago. I have an uncle who lives in town. He took care of me for a few years after my mom died, but we don't get along well so now I'm making due on my own."

Emiko nodded, studying the curtain. Earlier she'd seen only the sky blue color. Now she saw that the curtain also bore the image of a lake, set beneath a tranquil azure sky and a handful of playful white clouds.

"Do you get along with your brother?" Janice asked, stepping down from the ladder.

"Nathan and I ... we get along, alright, I guess," Emiko replied. "We fight sometimes, and sometimes he acts like he's my father, but we've been doing okay without our dad."

"Sounds to me like he cares about you."

"I guess," Emiko mumbled.

Janice smiled, examining her handiwork. "I'm sure he'll be happy to see you whenever he gets back."

"Of course," Emiko said. *If only Janice knew the truth.*

Janice picked up the step ladder. "It's almost time for lunch. Take a short break while I fix us a bite."

"Really? I can take a break?"

"Of course. You've been a big help. Just don't let the praise go to your head." Janice winked. "Come back in twenty."

Basking in her freedom, Emiko bounded from the office like a fawn prancing through a meadow. Upon entering her room, she heard her neighbors having an animated conversation. She quietly took a seat by the wall and put her ear against it to listen.

"Look at what I found," Leonard said. "A radio, and with a working battery, no less."

"Let's hope you don't break this one," Smitty said, wryly. "Where'd you find it?"

"In a house on the outskirts of town. I just had to step over a few skeletons to get it. There's so much junk sitting around in those suburban homes that the survivors here in Duluth could never begin to sort through it all."

"Have you dialed in the General yet?"

"No, I figured I'd wait for you."

"Good call."

The conversation fell silent. Emiko wished she could see what the two men were up to. They were likely fiddling with their newfound radio, but she had no way to be sure.

"HQ, do you copy?" Smitty finally broke the silence. "Private Smith, speaking. Also present is Private Redding. Could you patch us through to the General?"

There was a pause, then Smitty continued.

"This is Private Smith, sir. You sent me and my colleague, Private Leonard Redding, to look into activity in the Canadian oil fields."

There was another pause. Emiko realized that she could only hear half the conversation. Perhaps the radio wasn't loud enough to resonate through the walls.

"Yes, sir. We apologize for our unexpected silence. We had some radio trouble."

Another pause. Emiko was frustrated that she couldn't hear what the man on the other side, the General, was saying.

"We're currently in Duluth, sir. As for the oil, what we found was promising, but logistical issues involving transportation and distribution remain. We'd need to invest significant time and resources to develop a supply chain if we wanted to make the oil field viable."

A momentary silence.

"We have a small car with half a tank of gas, sir. We can get back to HQ but probably not much farther. How should we proceed?"

HQ? Headquarters? Emiko wished they'd reveal its location instead of speaking so vaguely.

"Of course, sir," Smitty said. "We'd be glad to remain here and work on recruitment. Duluth seems like a prime spot to bolster our numbers. Will that be all, sir?"

After another unheard response from the General, Leonard jumped into the conversation.

"Wait, sir! One more thing before you sign off. We saw the man you told us to look out for, sir."

Could it be? Emiko wondered. It would explain why they had exploded out of the bar after Beard.

"Oh, you mean we're not the first to have seen him?" Leonard asked, abandoning any hint of formality.

The ensuing silence was broken by a disappointed sigh from Smitty.

"Ah, yes, sir," Leonard said, apologetically. "Sorry, sir, I didn't mean to be so bold. It won't happen again, sir. I'm glad to hear you have the situation under control, sir."

"Anything else, sir?" Smitty asked, sounding eager to get his partner away from the radio.

After one final pause, the two men resuming talking between themselves.

"Dammit, Leonard, you were supposed to let me do the talking," Smitty chafed. "The General probably thinks we're two bumbling insubordinates now." Despite the wall separating Emiko from the two men, it was obvious that the respectful demeanor they'd adopted in talking to the General was now gone.

"He can't do much while we're way up here," Leonard replied. "Besides, he'll forget all about it if we bring in a few new recruits."

"You'd best hope so. Now, come on, let's get out of here. We got work to do."

"Where are we gonna start the recruitment drive?"

"Tonight we'll work the bars. Until then, we'll roam around Duluth and see what opportunities arise."

"Deal."

A moment later, Emiko heard the door click open and slam shut. Smitty and Leonard passed by her window, their shadows flitting across her room. Emiko waited until the men were a safe distance away before standing and flinging herself onto her bed.

Surprisingly, Emiko was beginning to appreciate her situation at the hotel. She was grateful to Janice for offering the room, the opportunity, and the friendly companionship. Still, as Emiko sat alone atop her bed — the softest bed she'd slept on in years — she felt herself growing restless.

Working at the hotel helped her realize how much being outdoors meant to her. Despite the fuss she made every time Nathan called her "The great huntress of Frontier View," she secretly relished the title.

Life at the hotel was good, but the wilderness was her home. How much longer could she wait, hoping to learn something useful from Smitty and Leonard? Emiko knew she would have to return to Frontier View eventually. Assuming no new leads cropped up, perhaps it would be best to make her homecoming sooner rather than later.

"Emiko, lunch is ready!" Janice's voice called from outside.

Emiko hopped to her feet, eagerly anticipating lunch. Soups, sandwiches, and fresh Minnesota summer salads were Janice's typical fare. Emiko enjoyed each crisp green leaf of salad and every tasty crumb of homemade bread. Emiko knew that when she did venture back to Frontier View, she'd have to again face the monotony of Pierre's protein-packed meat stews. Fortunately, for the time being that possibility remained just an "if."

Chapter 15

NATHAN AND JOHN passed through the lonely, desolate remains of Orr and continued northwest through forest and bog, upland and lowland. After a few days of tedious travel, they arrived at the edge of International Falls. A dilapidated, hand-carved sign beside the road declared the city to be the "Icebox of the Nation."

The noon sun hung high in the sky, its heat an unrelenting reminder that autumn hadn't yet come. The long journey was taking its toll. Feet hurt, legs ached, thoughts wandered. Even Mumford, steady as he was, slackened his pace as the day grew long.

As Nathan and John proceeded from the outskirts of the city toward the center, they encountered the familiar sights of a town abandoned. The houses had peeling paint, broken windows, sagging roofs, cracked driveways, and overgrown lawns. There was not a human soul in sight.

They passed a large, brick schoolhouse adjoined by a paved expanse. Two basketball hoops protruded from the blacktop, opposing each other like gunslingers facing off for a duel. Despite the passage of time, the faded white backboards and rusty chain nets were still intact.

A pair of deer bounded directly into the school through the open, unprotected main entrance, where heavy, steel doors would've once hung. Thick swaths of pale green moss clung to the building's orange brick exterior, complementing the confusion of weeds and wild sunflowers that sprang from the rooftop. The school had become a sanctuary for the flora and fauna of the north.

"Amazing how much the world has changed in just nine years," Nathan mused. "Nine years ago, there would've been kids chasing all around of this building." He wondered if speaking about that lost time was a sore point for John.

"It's August," John replied, gazing at the massive building. "Students would still be on summer vacation."

"Good point," Nathan said. Mindlessly, he kicked an egg-sized stone into the waist-high grass at the edge of the basketball court, rousing an irritated pair of field sparrows. Nathan watched the birds fly off down the street until losing them in the distance.

"So, what's the plan?" he asked. "Rainy Lake isn't far now."

"Let's find a place to sit down and eat."

Before long, Nathan and John happened upon an area of short grass in front of a quaint, ranch-style home with peeling yellow paint and a conspicuously unmatching red-shingled roof. Uninterested in scrounging up enough scrap wood for a campfire, Nathan and John resorted to backup rations — moose jerky and pilot biscuits.

As he gnawed on a particularly tough stick of jerky, Nathan noticed movement in the periphery of his vision. Turning quickly, he caught a glimpse of a small boy, poking his head out from the corner of the pink house across the street. The child made brief eye contact, then ducked back behind the house.

"Did you see that?" Nathan asked.

"See what?" John shook his head.

"Not sure. I'm gonna check it out," Nathan said, stuffing the remaining jerky into his mouth as he trotted to the other side of the street. He approached the house cautiously, advancing slowly creeping across the lawn. Peering around the corner, he found nothing — the child had vanished.

Where could the little guy have gone? Nathan wondered, surveying the backyard. The pink paint on the wooden siding looked like it had been freshly applied, and two of the rear windows appeared to be in much better condition than the others, as though they had been recently replaced.

"Ooof," Nathan uttered, wincing at a pain in his toe. Frowning, he glanced at his feet. His big toe had accidentally discovered one of several cement blocks that framed a pair of cellar doors. He noticed that the grass and dandelions were matted along one side of the doors. It didn't look like the work of nature's hand. Perhaps International Falls wasn't as deserted as they'd thought.

Nathan grabbed the rusty metal ring affixed to one of the doors and pulled. The hinges creaked loudly as he rested the wooden door against the frame. Staying well outside the view of anyone below, he took a step back and pressed his spine flat against the house and listened intently for any evidence of life below.

Nathan's heart throbbed intently. Long moments passed. Nothing.

A crow cawed raucously overhead, causing Nathan's arm hair to stand erect. Waiting was only breaking his composure. Steeling himself, he called down into the dark abyss:

"I know you're down there."

No response.

"I'm unarmed," he added, trying to control the wavering in his voice.

Faint mumbles rose from the cellar. After several moments, Nathan grew impatient.

"I can hear you," he announced, with growing confidence. "I'm unarmed. I just wanna talk."

A throaty, decidedly masculine voice called back. "We could smell your godforsaken trail of moose crap from the next town over. We saw you come into town, armed to the teeth! We're getting darn sick and tired of you and your kind passing through our peaceful community."

"Me and my kind?"

"Yeah, you soldier types."

Nathan shook his head. "I'm no soldier. I'm just a kid from Frontier View, trying to find help for a friend."

"And what kind of help are you hoping to find in International Falls?" There was a hint of surprise in the man's voice.

Nathan considered how best to explain. Out of context, his story would sound wild and absurd. He and John had come all this way based on an unconfirmed story from the mouth of

Ramses Brushnell, a man as trustworthy as a compass with a magnet glued to its underside.

"You two alone?" the man asked, as Nathan had still not responded.

"My partner and our tvapa are out around front," Nathan called down. "I'm the only one here in back."

The voices below debated.

"Alright, here's the plan," the man shouted up. "Step in front of the entrance and keep your hands where we can see then. We'll come up to meet you."

Could Nathan trust these unseen strangers enough to confront them unarmed? It wasn't too late to summon John for help.

He sighed. A little trust could go a long way ... or it could leave him a buckshot riddled corpse.

"I'm going to step in front of the entryway now," he hollered down the cellar hole. "Are you ready?"

"Ready when you are," the voice shot back.

Nathan stepped away from the house, raised his hands in the air, and cautiously proceeded to the cellar's entrance. He peered into the darkness. Were there two people down there? Three? Six? His mind raced as he waited for the subterranean denizens to come topside.

The outline of a man appeared, his face hidden in the shadows. His shoes scraped softly against the wooden stairs as he ascended. Nathan tensed at the sight of the shotgun in the man's hands, yet stood his ground.

"Jeez, you weren't joking when you said you were just a scrawny kid." The sunlight revealed the man's features as he drew closer. His face was narrow with high cheek bones and a hint of gray stubble. Atop his head of thick, graying hair was a tattered black hat with the word "Bobcat" embroidered in yellow. The man warily scanned the immediate area. Satisfied, he turned his gazed to Nathan.

"Scrawny?" Nathan said, annoyed, keeping his hands in the air.

The man shrugged and turned his body slightly. "Come on up — it's safe!" he shouted into the cellar. Two figures emerged from the darkness. Nathan recognized one as the boy he'd seen first. The other was a woman, perhaps 35, with long, dark hair.

The man scrutinized Nathan from head to toe.

"Put your hands down and relax. We were enjoying a little sunshine, but when we saw you approach we hurried underground. Thought you were two of them goons — our mistake. It's not often we get visitors here."

"Visitors are a rarity everywhere these days," Nathan said, rubbing the back of his neck. "Speaking of goons, do these goons you mentioned wear green vests?"

"Always! Sounds like you've run into them."

"They've given me and my partner some trouble, too."

"Well, if you can spare the time, let's have a chat about it." The man smiled. "Care to come inside for a cup of herbal tea?"

Nathan nodded. "Sounds great. Is it alright if my friend joins us?"

The young boy tugged anxiously at the man's shirt. "Grandpa, is his friend the scary bearded man?"

"Now now, Thomas, remember what I told you about judging a book by its cover? Though I guess even I'm guilty of doing so, at times," the man added with an awkward chuckle.

"But people aren't books, Grandpa."

"No, people are far more precious."

The boy nodded, then stepped back and wrapped his arms around the waist of the woman — his mother, Nathan guessed.

"I hope you won't judge John by his gruff appearance," Nathan said, heading back around the house to get John. "He's a little rough around the edges, but he's a straight shooter."

Chapter 16

JUST AS JOHN was preparing to look for him, Nathan reappeared from behind the house with three companions. After cursory introductions, Victor showed Nathan where to tie up Mumford and the group went inside. Removing their shoes entryway, John and Nathan were led into the kitchen. A luminous shaft of sunlight streamed through a wide, two-pane window. The black and white tiled floor glowed like a shiny new checkerboard in the bright light.

John sat at a table, watching as the old man, Victor, and his daughter, Georgia, prepared afternoon tea. The young boy, Thomas, hid in the living room, occasionally risking an apprehensive glance into the kitchen at John.

"So, what of your families?" Victor asked as he tended the fire in the cast-iron stove.

"I lost my mom to the Desolation," Nathan said, betraying little emotion as he recounted the event that had long since passed. "But I still have a sister back home in Frontier View."

"And your father?" Victor asked.

"That … I lost him a bit more recently," Nathan said, his shoulders slumping.

"I'm sorry to hear that." Victor paused a moment, granting the weight of Nathan's loss the respectful consideration it deserved. "Me and my daughter, Georgia here, we were immune to the virus. My wife and Georgia's husband weren't so fortunate." Heaving a tired sigh, Victor smiled meekly. "However, God smiled upon us and saw fit to pass my immunity down two generations to little Thomas over there.

He was born in the spring after the Desolation, a final gift from the departed."

John's thoughts drifted as Victor and Nathan continued chatting. He'd been in a coma during the Desolation, and stories from that time didn't resonate with him like they did with other survivors. Like the Kennedy assassination, 9/11, and the Great SoCal Earthquake of 2023, the Desolation was an event that had crystallized in the collective mind of the people, a troubled time from which everyone had emerged with their own personal memory to share — everyone but John.

That said, he'd still suffered losses. Would it have been worth seeing so much pain and death, had it given him a few final days to say goodbye to his friends and family? It was a decision no man should have to make, yet he would have taken the extra time without a second's hesitation. His time with the Marines had taught him to appreciate the present. Back in his active service days, when he'd left for duty he'd done so knowing that each and every goodbye could be his last. After all of those farewells, he never expected that he'd be the one left standing in the end.

"John?" Victor said.

"Yeah?" John looked up.

"How about you?" Victor offered a cautious smile.

"I was the sole survivor."

Victor hung his head. "I'm sorry to hear that."

"Don't be. What's done is done."

With a nod, Victor placed an aluminum tea kettle on the stove top and took a seat at the table. John looked around the kitchen. Georgia had moved to another room. Thomas was staring at him again. As soon as their eyes met, the young boy dove back out of sight.

"So, you said you came to International Falls to look for help?" Victor asked.

Neither John nor Nathan answered immediately. The kitchen grew dark as a cloud passed in front of the sun. Noting the change, John gratefully remembered how kind the weather had been to them on the journey thus far. A Minnesota summer could change colors faster than a mother bear could chase a man up a tree.

From the other room came the sound of wooden blocks tumbling to the floor, followed immediately by exuberant squeals of delight.

"We're headed to Mallard Island," Nathan said, taking the initiative. The more the two had traveled together, the more Nathan had become comfortable with handling the conversational duties. The change didn't go unappreciated by John.

"Is that right?" Victor's eyes widened. "You're not far now. Ten miles by road, then a mile by water. I used to belong to a group of volunteers that maintained the island — winterizing the buildings, keeping the docks in good repair, cleaning out the latrines, that sort of thing."

Nathan sat up in his chair. "So, you must know quite a bit about the island?"

"You bet I do. Used to be owned by a fellow named Ernest Oberholtzer. After he died, a foundation was formed to protect the island and his legacy. I was an active member of the group for many years, until the late 2010s. Around then, a bunch of military folk — U.S. Navy, as I recall — started using the area for training operations. Huge controversy at the time. We locals didn't like it, of course, but the military brass pleaded 'national security' and the ballgame was over. The world was a crazy place in those final years before the Desolation."

"I was young, but I remember my dad complaining about similar issues at the university," Nathan offered.

"The University of Minnesota?" Victor asked.

"Yeah, he was a chemistry professor there, in Minneapolis."

"Must've been a smart fellow."

Nathan nodded grimly. Victor took it as a sign to move on.

"I haven't been out to the island in over a dozen years. I know a few of our volunteers persevered, though. They came to an uneasy truce of sorts with the military and continued to maintain the island after I'd moved on. That being said, I highly doubt anyone's visited the island since the Desolation." Victor paused for a moment, scratching the tip of his nose. "Honestly, I can't imagine what you'd find there that would be of use to you, unless you're into rare books. Ober had an extensive collection. Must be over 10,000 volumes lining the shelves, about everything from the air-speed velocity of an unladen African swallow to the inner workings of the Norwegian parliament."

This Ober guy sounds like a real egghead, John thought, rubbing his beard. He maintained his silence, however, so as not to offend.

"What we're looking for is health-related. A friend of ours has a medical issue that isn't responding to conventional treatment. We were told Mallard Island may hold a solution," Nathan explained without hesitation. While truthful, his explanation left much unstated. Nathan was learning the fine art of diplomacy, it seemed.

Victor scratched his head. "Well, I'm not sure what you'll find, but in any case, I'm willing to take you there. Been itching to see the place again."

"That won't be necessary," John said, leaning back in his chair.

"You sure?" Victor asked.

"I'm sure. Those 'soldier-types' you mentioned earlier — I think they might have a connection to Mallard Island."

Victor nodded. "That right?"

"Our info came from a young soldier with ambitions of revolution."

"Revolution? In Minnesota? You must be joking." Victor furrowed his brow. "There's nothing to revolt against, and even if there were, I don't see how anyone could round up enough willing bodies to mount a revolution."

"It might look that way from up here, but you'd think differently if you saw Duluth. The city is growing like wildfire and establishing itself as the capital of the Republic of Minnesota. The government's rule is far from secure, though, and a power-hungry warmonger with group of disillusioned young men could stir up trouble."

"Sounds a little farfetched," Victor replied.

"I'm speculating, yes," John said with a shrug. "But I don't trust these men in green vests. It's best if you stay clear of them. You need to look after your daughter and grandson. Let us handle Mallard Island."

The tea kettle whistled shrilly, prompting Georgia's hasty return to the kitchen. With a red, hand-knit oven mitt, she poured the boiling water into a ceramic teapot to steep. Judging from the smell, John guessed the tea ingredients included peppermint and wild rice.

"You'll stay for tea," Georgia stated rather than asked.

"I don't see why not," John replied. Though eager to get to Mallard Island, he had warmed to Georgia and Victor and didn't want to decline their hospitality.

"How many people live in International Falls?" Nathan wondered out loud.

"Maybe forty, fifty, scattered about the town," Victor answered. "My family had been living here since well before the Desolation, and we didn't see any reason to leave after the tragedy. Lots of other families felt the same — good people here. The folks living in Fort Frances, our sister city on the other side of the Canadian border, moved down this way too. The communities really came together. When you can't fill up your truck at a gas station and hopscotch across town, living far apart just doesn't make sense. We came to realize that pretty quickly."

Victor rambled on, delighted to have a captive audience in the curious young man. Soon, Georgia arrived with the teapot and poured a cup for John. "Be careful — it's hot," she whispered. John smiled and silently mouthed the words "thank you" as he carefully gripped the steaming cup. After sipping to check the temperature, he turned his attention back to the conversation.

"Is anyone left in Fort Frances?" Nathan asked, also accepting a cup of tea from Georgia.

"It's possible there are folks living there," Victor said, "but as far as I know it's a ghost town. To tell it straight, I don't think there was any particular reason we gathered in International Falls instead of Fort Frances. Just happened to work out that way."

"I wouldn't be so sure. Everything happens for a reason," Georgia jumped in, taking a seat at the table. She delicately balanced her steaming cup of tea. "This is where we're destined to be, among good company. I can't believe God would have left such a thing up to chance."

John rubbed his left shoulder. If a benevolent higher being did exist, that being had made a peculiar choice in selecting John to be the recipient of such a powerful gift. Or perhaps the being had bestowed the arm as a curse ...

"You sure you don't want to stay the night?" Victor asked. "Bald Rock Point is where you'll want to put your boat in. That's still a good half-day's hike from here. Even if you got there before nightfall, you'd still have a lot of lake standing between you and Mallard Island. Rainy Lake is huge, and especially dicey when the wind is up. You'll need to be careful."

"What do you think?" Nathan asked John. "The island isn't going anywhere."

John nodded. "I suppose."

"Glad to hear it," Victor said. "Georgia and I will fix a few provisions and send you on your way tomorrow morning. In the meantime, make yourselves at home."

"Can do," John said. "Just one more thing: do you have an awl?"

"Need to do some leather-work?"

"Just need to adjust my belt. A knife would work, but an awl would be better."

Victor nodded. "I'm sure I have one around here somewhere. I'll see what I can dig up."

* * *

For dinner, Georgia served chicken noodle soup, complete with fresh chicken, homemade noodles, and an assortment of garden vegetables. Sides of mashed potatoes and summer squash rounded out the meal. In contrast to the hard-as-granite biscuits and tough-as-moose-hide jerky that Nathan and John had endured on the road, the dinner felt like a homecoming feast fit for a pair conquering heroes. The truth, however, was that Nathan had never been farther from home.

After everyone had finished eating, Victor went down to the basement. He returned triumphantly with a bottle of Johnnie Walker in hand. Receiving visitors from out of town was a rare treat, and he insisted that the three men share a drink to commemorate the good old days.

Nathan took a tiny sip of the whisky, recoiling at the nip of fire against his tongue. The good old days didn't taste as pleasant as he'd expected. He set his glass back on the table, where it remained while John and Victor savored a few more shots. Nathan and John then bid Victor a fond goodnight, and Georgia led them to the guest room.

A wooden lamp, shaped like a black bear climbing a honey tree, rested on the table between two beds. Its flame cast soft shadows across the simple furniture — a caned chair, a one-drawer desk, and a knotty pine bookshelf.

"I'm glad we found friendly folks to stay with tonight," Nathan said, taking a seat on the edge of his bed and letting his legs dangle.

From the other bed, John gave a grunt and a nod in reply. Nathan looked on as John unbuckled his belt and pulled it free from the loops of his well-worn blue jeans. Clutching Victor's awl firmly in one hand, John punched a new hole in the brown leather belt.

Nathan cocked his head. Had John been losing weight? Though the beard made it hard to discern with certainty, his cheeks did seem a little thin, his face more gaunt than it had been. Nathan considered asking about it, before deciding that John's reply would most likely be another of his one syllable grunts.

After testing the new hole in his belt, John undressed and got ready for bed. Nathan followed suit, stripping down to his underwear. John then extinguished the lamp.

Faint beams of moonlight, partially obscured by clouds, illuminated the room. Nathan stared out at the stars as they bobbed and weaved behind the thin cloud cover. Was his father up there somewhere, looking back down at him? Victor had asked about family during tea. Nathan missed his family deeply. Not only his father, but also Emiko and even Pierre.

"John, I can't sleep."

After a moment of silence, John responded.

"What's up, kid?"

"Do you know what happened last time I left Frontier View?"

"I've heard bits and pieces."

"Well, you know, last year I took my father to Duluth ..."

"Go on."

"He was sick, really sick. Far beyond what Cynthia could deal with. So we went to Duluth to see what the doctors would say. After some tests, we found out that he had late stage stomach cancer."

Nathan waited to see if John would jump in. When John didn't, he continued.

"My father lost his fighting spirit when he heard the news. He spent his final weeks in that hospital room. I stayed with him. It was rough, the darkest time of my life. There was nothing I could do. Ever since, I've questioned why we left Frontier View to seek help in Duluth. Why couldn't I have just let him die peacefully, among friends at home?"

John didn't offer an immediate response. In the distance, a Great Horned Owl hooted somberly.

"You can't blame yourself," John stated, his voice firm. "You wanted to help. There was no way you could've known in advance what was going to happen."

"But —"

"So you made a choice, and you know what? It didn't work out. But given the information you had it was the best choice. So now you can either be victim of that choice, or you can move on with your life. Your father isn't coming back either way. He'd want you to look forward, not back."

"How?"

"Keep moving. Keep fighting. Keep doing the right thing. And never quit, no matter how long the odds are, no matter how hard they try to stop you."

Nathan sighed. "I wish I had your courage, John."

"You were damn courageous the other night in Duluth."

"I guess. But even then, I needed help."

John didn't respond immediately. Nathan again peered out the window. Though the moon was now fully hidden, its silver light still sharply illuminated the edges of the dark cloud bank.

"We all need help, sometimes," John offered.

Nathan continued to stare out the window. His eyelids grew heavy as his body relaxed.

"You still awake?" John asked. The question went unanswered.

Nathan felt at ease. As he drifted off to sleep, he thought he heard John roll over in bed and mumble, "I wish I had my courage, too, kid."

Chapter 17

NATHAN, JOHN, AND VICTOR arrived at Rainy Lake late the next morning. Despite John's protests, Victor had insisted on accompanying his guests to the lake, offering to guide Mumford back to International Falls and take care of the tvapa as one of his own until the two men returned from their island adventure.

Once the three men came to a halt at the put-in, Nathan unhitched Mumford from the cart and turned the reins over to Victor.

"You two sure you'll be alright?" Victor asked.

"We'll be back before you know it," Nathan replied with a confident smile. "I hope Mumford doesn't give you too much trouble."

"My family will be awaiting your safe return. May God be with you." Having said his piece, Victor tugged at Mumford's reins and guided the beast back down the trail from which they'd come.

After watching Victor depart, Nathan went to unload their gear and ready the canoe. As he dug through his supplies, he noticed John scrunching his nose and glowering in disgust at the sole of one of his boots. On the ground just beside John was a flattened clump of tvapa dung, stamped with a fresh boot print.

"Frankenmeese," John muttered. "The mongrel must've left that pile of crap there on purpose. Knew my boot would find it."

"Really? I thought you and Mumford were getting along better recently."

"Hardly. As we speak, the frankenmoose army is undoubtedly plotting to overthrow what remains of human civilization."

Nathan rolled his eyes, then turned his attention to the wide expanse of Rainy Lake. The lake was one of the largest in Minnesota. It was no surprise he couldn't see the far shore. In contrast to Lake Superior's endless blue surface, however, Rainy Lake boasted a host of lush green islands, which glistened in the sun like veins of precious ore protruding from a vast sheet of bedrock. On blustery days the lee side of those islands provided the only safe haven from the full brunt of the wind.

Though still early, Nathan and John decided to have lunch. The morning's trek had aroused their appetites and they were anxious to see what Georgia had packed for them.

"These pork sandwiches are great," Nathan enthused. "I hope we get one more chance to enjoy Victor and Gloria's hospitality on the way home."

"Agreed." John stared out at the lake, obviously lost in thought.

"Say, John, I know I asked you this before, but have you given any more thought to why Ramses wanted you to come here?"

"I have, but I haven't made much headway. Too many things we don't know." John set the remaining half of his sandwich on his lap. "We know these men are after me. We also know they're after oil. If I were planning a revolution, those are two things I'd want on my side."

"Why don't these people, whoever they are, just ask for your help?"

"Maybe they just want the gizmo that's grafted to my body. Or, perhaps they've concluded that I'd never join them. They haven't exactly endeared me to their cause. Another possibility is that there's a larger prize to be had and my arm is merely the key to finding it." John offered a shrug and picked up his sandwich.

"It's that last possibility that I'm worried about," Nathan said.

John swallowed the last bite of his sandwich and patted his belly.

"I'm not sure I have time to worry," John stated cryptically. He rose to ready the canoe for departure, leaving Nathan to finish lunch alone.

Is there something he's not telling me? Nathan thought back to the night before, when he'd watched John poke a new hole in his belt. Something was amiss; Nathan just wasn't sure what it was. After downing the rest of his sandwich, he went to give John a hand.

Nathan and John securely strapped down the packs into the canoe with rope. They then stepped into the boat, Nathan taking the bow and John the stern. They gripped their paddles and pushed off.

Despite the heavy packs, the aluminum canoe cut gracefully through the water, responding eagerly to the strokes of Nathan's paddle. Though only their second time paddling together, Nathan and John quickly found a comfortable rhythm and progressed rapidly across the lake. For balance they paddled on opposite sides of the canoe, switching sides at John's command.

"How long do you think it will take to get to Mallard Island?" Nathan asked.

"Should take less than an hour," John responded.

Nathan nodded, biting his lip apprehensively. Though he was a skilled canoeist, Rainy Lake was the widest body of water he'd ever attempted to cross. Its vast scale made him uneasy, and paddling in silence didn't help calm his nerves. Still, not wanting to bother John with idle chitchat, Nathan did his best to focus fully on his paddling technique, keeping his posture erect and turning his shoulders and torso with each stroke.

Nathan hadn't the slightest idea what awaited them on Mallard Island. Why had Ramses lured them here? What did the remote island have to do with John's arm? Would they find a cure for John's distressed, sudden bouts of illness? Nathan yearned for answers like a field of dry, brown grass looked forward to a summer squall.

As they traveled farther from the shore Nathan's heartbeat quickened, pulsating against the grip of his paddle. He took a deep, calming breath and rested his paddle on the gunwale.

"Now's not the time for a break," John said. "Take a look at the sky."

Nathan looked up. Dark, angry cumulus clouds were racing in from the west. How had he not noticed earlier? He felt John's powerful strokes propelling the canoe forward. With a nervous gulp, he tightened his grip and redoubled his efforts, applying the full strength of his back and core muscles to the now critical task at hand.

"Stay calm up there, kid," John said. "We have a ways to go yet. I don't want either of us petering out before we arrive."

Gale force winds swept across the lake, causing its surface to swell and billow. Spray filled the air. The swells peaked into frothing whitecaps, battering the boat from side to side, breaking over the bow, and sloshing into the hull.

"Dead ahead, I see it!" John called out, struggling to be heard through the swirling wind. Squinting, Nathan could just make out the island in the distance — a small strip of bedrock, sandwiched between menacing black clouds above and jagged, crashing waves below.

"Paddle!" John shouted. Nathan obliged, pushing his shoulders and arms to their limit.

As they neared the island, rain pelted down from the sky. The cold hard drops hammered at Nathan's eyes, adding to the rising water level in the canoe. Neither he nor John were wearing life jackets. Their options: paddle or drown.

Accumulating water weighed down the boat, making it sluggish and unstable. Though their destination was only a few hundred meters away, no matter how frantically they paddled they could pull no closer to the elusive island. Nathan's muscles started to cramp, his strokes becoming erratic.

"Push!" John screamed.

Tapping into reserves he didn't know he had, Nathan paddled furiously despite the cramping. Rain crashed down like volleys of bullets, assaulting them from every direction. They steered the canoe toward a rocky inlet that offered protection.

As they entered the shallow inlet a rogue wave swept under the waterlogged canoe, sending it hurtling toward the rocks. Nathan flailed through the air, nearly flying from his seat as the canoe came slamming down against a partially submerged boulder. The harsh, sickening sound of crumpling aluminum rang out.

"She's going down! Grab your pack and get out!" John shouted.

Nathan leapt from the boat. In his mad rush, he bashed his shin on a protruding rock. His feet found the uneven bottom of the inlet, the water swirling at his waist. Battling to ignore the acute pain in his leg, he spun around, untying his pack from the thwart of the canoe and slinging it onto his back. He rushed for shore, trusting that John could make his own way. He struggled to maintain his balance, twice nearly losing his footing on the slippery rocks below. With a final desperate lunge he threw himself ashore, collapsing on the wet grass utterly exhausted.

They'd arrived on Mallard Island.

Nathan's heart pounded in his ears. Between the thumps he heard the slosh of John approaching.

"The good news is that we're here," John said. "The bad news is that our ship is sunk, and there's no way we're swimming back across that lake."

Nathan wrestled his pack off and rolled over onto this back, looking up at John. "We saved all the gear?"

"Except for the paddles, not that we need them anymore," John replied. "Hopefully our waterproof packs did their job."

"What about the canoe?"

John shook his head. "Alumacraft canoes are common. We can find another one just like it in International Falls."

Nathan closed his eyes. The aluminum boat was easily replaceable, but its sentimental value was not. The canoe had been his father's, and Nathan had always done his best to treat it with respect. Now it was gone, just like his dad.

"You ready to explore this place?" John asked.

As he tried to rise, Nathan let out a loud groan. His adrenaline rush had subsided, and pain gnawed at his wounded shin.

John knelt beside him to assess the damage. "Did you break anything?" he asked.

"I don't think so. It just hurts like hell."

"Roll up your pant leg."

Nathan obliged, tugging at the leg of his jeans and exposing his shin, allowing John to take a closer look.

"It doesn't look broken," John said. He reached to touch the shin, causing Nathan to gasp in pain.

"You probably just have a bad bruise. It'll hurt, and in a couple of hours it'll swell up, but you should be able to stand on it without any trouble." John rose to his feet and held out a hand to Nathan. "In fact, I bet you can walk it off. How about we get out of here and find some shelter?"

Nathan agreed readily. He accepted the proffered hand and let John pull him to his feet. Surprisingly, as unsympathetic as John's advice had sounded, he'd been right: Walking did help take his mind off the pain.

Chapter 18

SEEKING SHELTER FROM the driving rain, John and Nathan hurried toward the nearest building, a long, cabin-like structure with white wooden siding. Above the entryway, the word "Wannigan" was painted in faded black letters. Following behind Nathan, John ducked inside the building, letting the screened door slam shut behind him.

The door led into a room about the size of an office cubicle, with windows overlooking the lake. Along the walls were shelves of books, mostly old hardcovers. To one side was a small staircase that led down to a larger room. Nathan had already ventured down the stairs, apparently unhindered by his injured shin.

Lightning flashed, casting elongated shadows across the room. The boom of thunder that followed reverberated through the late afternoon air. Heaving a tired sigh, John descended, stooping so as not to hit his head. At the bottom of the staircase, he found Nathan standing in the middle of the room, shivering as he removed his sopping wet clothes. Nathan's hands shook as he slipped into a dry black t-shirt and blue jeans, taken from the dry interior of his backpack.

The lower level appeared to be the building's primary room. To one side was a dinner table large enough to sit a dozen hungry men, surrounded by handcrafted oak chairs. On the other side was a full kitchen, complete with a two-burner stove top and a large gas oven. Stacks of canned goods were piled along the back wall, collecting dust.

John set down his pack and dug out a wrinkled blue plaid flannel shirt and a pair of jeans to replace his water drenched red plaid and denim attire. After he finished buttoning his shirt, he took two large chunks of deer jerky from the pack and offered one to Nathan. The two men sat at the table, nibbling at the jerky in silence. They both needed the rest.

Nathan was the first to stand. He began to explore the room. His gait exhibited no ill effects from the blow to his leg.

"Take a look at this," he said, flipping through the pages of a book at the end of the table. "It looks like a guest book. The last entry is initialed HSO, dated October 12th, 2025."

"About two years before the Desolation, right?" John said, rising from the table.

"Right, which means that it wasn't the Desolation itself that stopped people from coming here."

"Well, Victor did mention that controversy regarding the government's use of the lake. His explanation was scant on details, but I'd bet there's a connection."

John's eyes shifted toward the far end of the table, where a collection of wine bottles stood in a row along the wall. Examining the bottles, he found that most were Napa Valley reds from 2022 and 2023.

"There's a map over here," Nathan called for John's attention, pointing to a well-worn poster on the wall with edges that curled inward. "Looks like there are ten major buildings on the island."

John stood beside Nathan, eyeing the poster. The island was long and narrow, running fairly straight from east to west. The building they presently stood inside, the Wannigan, was toward the eastern end of the island. There were nine other buildings:

Artist's House
Bird House
Cedar Bark
Cook's House
Front House
Japanese House
Library
Ober's House
Winter House

"What's that?" Nathan said, pointing to a fist-sized cube that jutted out from the wall beside the map. After squinting closely at the face of the cube, he took it in one hand and squeezed tightly. Nothing happened. He tried again, this time wrapping both hands around it. Same result.

"I had to try," he said with an amused shrug. "I think it's for you."

John stepped to the cube and felt its smooth, dark chrome finish. He didn't recognize the metal alloy it was made of. Examining its front face, he discovered a few words of laser-etched text:

Should you come bearing arm(s), crush me.

John furrowed his brow as he palmed the front face of the cube in his left hand, extended his fingers around it, and squeezed with unhinged bionic force. Beads of sweat gathered on his forehead. The cube's metal alloy was stronger than steel, harder than diamond. John closed his eyes to keep his growing wooziness at bay. The cube began to submit to the will of his fingers, and when the metal could resist his efforts no further the sides of the cube imploded. A portion of the cube remained affixed to the wall, while the bottom half broke into fragments that clattered against the wooden floorboards.

"Look!" Nathan exclaimed, pointing at a small yellow square of paper that drifted through the air, like a leaf falling from a tree.

Shaking off his lightheadedness, John dropped to one knee to pick up the paper — a yellow post-it note. It bore a short message, handwritten in heavy black pen. Struggling to decipher the sloppy cursive writing, he read aloud:

To the far east
above the ground
follow the owl's gaze
a clue is found

"A poem?" Nathan said.

"A riddle. Do you like riddles?" John extended his arm, offering the note to the kid.

"Only if they involve a pocket and a precious, evil ring that renders its wearer invisible."

John squinted at the kid. "Huh?"

"Not a fan of classic high fantasy literature, I guess? Let me see if I can find a pencil and paper so I can make a copy of the riddle."

"A copy? Why?"

"There may be more clues. If so, I'd like to have them all together in one place. Also, we should treat the original clue with care, just in case the post-it note itself serves a dual purpose."

"You really do like riddles, don't you?"

Nathan didn't reply as he searched the room. After finding a spiral-bound notebook and a pencil, he took the note from John and jotted down its contents. Once finished, he stuck it to the wall next to the remains of the metal cube.

"So, what do you think it means?" John asked, rubbing 'his' chin as he studied the map on the wall. "'Far east,' as in the Orient, would mean Japanese House, right?" He pointed to the building, on the western tip of the island.

"Maybe, although usually when referring to East Asia, 'far east' is capitalized. So, it could be Japanese House, but it could also be Front House, the easternmost building," Nathan speculated, indicating the structure on the far right side of the map.

"You think our riddler would've considered that?"

Nathan shrugged. "Only one way to find out. Besides, Front House is a shorter walk."

"If the scale of this map is correct, the whole island isn't much of a walk," John countered. "I think we should —"

Lightning streaked through the windows of the Wannigan, followed immediately by an earthshaking roar. Gradually, the thunder faded to a dull, deep-throated rumble, while the wind-whipped rain continued to lash the building's exterior.

"You were saying ..." Nathan trailed off.

"Alright, we'll do things your way. Let's check out Front House."

"Did you bring a raincoat?"

"No." John shook his head. "You?"

"Yeah, let me put it on," Nathan said, ferreting through his pack. Meanwhile, John looked around the Wannigan, quickly finding what he sought — a lantern. He gripped it by the base and gently shook it back and forth. He was rewarded by the welcome slosh of kerosene. After checking the wick, he attempted to light it with a match from a box of kitchen stick matches near the stove. Three spent matches later, the wick finally cooperated. The lantern's initial sputtering threads of light grew into a steady luminous sphere.

"Ready?" John turned to Nathan, now clad in a bright yellow raincoat.

"You bet."

"Sure you don't need to put on your little yellow rain boots, too?" John's lips curved into an easy smile.

"Funny." Nathan frowned. "Let's go."

* * *

Moving swiftly through the driving rain, the pair approached Front House, a large, rustic two-story structure with a steeply slanted shingled roof. It was less than a hundred meters east of the Wannigan, which suggested that the island was quite compact, just as they had initially conjectured.

Once inside, Nathan shook his arms and stomped his feet, throwing off the water that had collected on his rain jacket. John followed behind, carrying the lantern and showing no concern about his saturated clothing.

"You could at least wipe the mud off your boots," Nathan said.

With a grunt, John dragged his bulky footwear across the welcome mat by the door.

"Mind if I take the lantern?" Nathan asked. John handed it to him without complaint.

The shadows fled from the lamplight, revealing the room's features. The floorboards were warped and discolored with age, matching the yellowed wallpaper that covered the walls. A hearth occupied the center of the far wall, no doubt having proved handy for staving off the fierce cold of Northwoods winters. Stacks of hardbound books cluttered the floor.

In addition to the front door there were two other exits: a trapdoor staircase that hung opposite the entryway and an open door frame to the side of the hearth. Nathan stepped through the open door frame and peered into the adjoining room. The modest light from his lamp illuminated every corner of the small room. Inside, he found only a piano and more books, most of which appeared to be musical scores.

"What do you think that riddle meant by the 'owl's gaze'?" he asked, returning to the first room.

"Don't ask me. You're the one who wanted to come here," John said.

Nathan remained silent, pondering the riddle. They were already above ground and the building didn't appear to have a basement. Perhaps, then, the clue was meant to direct them to the second floor? As Nathan's contemplated, lightning flashed twice in quick succession, followed a few seconds later by the rumble of retreating thunder.

"Let's go upstairs," he said, heading for the staircase. The narrow stairs creaked, warning him to step lightly and give the aged boards their due respect. When he reached the top of the staircase, he heard a sharp crack and spun on his heels.

"Hammersnap!" John exclaimed. His leg had disappeared into the newly-created hole in the staircase and his shoulder was braced against the wall. By the time Nathan could step down to offer his hand, John had already extracted himself from the broken stair.

I guess he doesn't need my help, Nathan thought, raising the lantern to better reveal the layout of the upper room. One corner was furnished with two metal frame beds. The beds were separated by an elegant handcrafted nightstand, upon which lay a pair of round, horn-rimmed glasses. Above the nightstand was a window. Raindrops rapped furiously against its glass pane.

Along the far wall, three shelves bravely supported crowded rows of books. Drawing closer, Nathan browsed through the titles, most of which were American and British literary fiction from the first half of the twentieth century. He thought to comment on the abundance of books but decided against stating the obvious in John's presence.

"So, where is the owl?" John asked, tapping his foot impatiently.

"I don't see it," Nathan answered. Had his intuition failed him? Scanning the walls again with his lantern, he failed to find an owl, living or dead.

John gestured down the staircase. "To Japanese House, then?"

"Wait." Nathan held up his hand, signaling for John to give him a moment. He stepped thoughtfully over to the nightstand and looked closely at the pair of horned-rimmed glasses. The thick lenses were turned downward, resting on the wooden surface. Setting down his lantern, he opened the drawer of the nightstand.

At first glance the drawer appeared empty. Nathan reached inside, turned his wrist upward, and felt above the drawer. His fingers brushed against a shred of paper, affixed to the rough, unfinished wood surface. Carefully, he removed it and brought it to the light. It was another small yellow post-it note, with cursive scrawl that matched the writing on the first clue.

"How'd you think to look there?" John asked.

"Owl-eyes," Nathan explained, holding up the horn-rimmed glasses with his other hand. "They were gazing down, into the drawer."

"Well played. What's it say?"

"Oh, right." Nathan set down the glasses and picked up the lantern, holding it close to the note. He read aloud:

In the cold of winter
beside the fire
beyond this side of paradise
lies your heart's desire

"Another riddle?" John groaned.

Nathan pursed his lips, then took out the pencil and spiral notebook he'd carried from the Wannigan and transcribed the second clue. After he finished copying, he stuck the note on top of the nightstand, beside the glasses.

John rubbed his beard. "So, what do you make of this one?"

"Well," Nathan said, scratching his head. "One of the buildings is called Winter House, but I can't remember which one it is off hand. Let's go take another look at the map."

"Deal," John said with a nod.

* * *

After swinging by the Wannigan to double-check the map, John and Nathan made their way west to Winter House. Following behind Nathan, who still held the lantern, John stepped out of the rain and into the cabin. This building was cozier than Front House. In the dim light, John imagined an old man spending the cold winter nights parked comfortably in the corner rocking chair, immersed in a well-worn book. The room's austere furnishings consisted of two small wooden beds, a one-drawer nightstand with a lantern atop, and a heavy hardwood table supplied with two caned oak chairs.

"The fireplace is over here," Nathan said, his face aglow with lantern light.

John stood back and watched Nathan pace across the room, his steps silenced by the carpet underfoot. While he was well schooled in combat strategy and had an intuitive understanding of politics and psychology, John readily admitted that riddles weren't his forte. If the kid wanted to take charge of the investigation, he saw no reason to interfere.

"Alright, so we found the fireplace," he said. "What's next?"

"The clue mentions 'this side of paradise,'" Nathan said, turning to the bookshelf beside the fireplace.

"*This Side of Paradise*? That's a famous novel, right?"

"Yeah, by F. Scott Fitzgerald. Have you read it?"

"I read the SparkNotes in high school," John said. As a teenager, he'd prioritized playing football and cruising in his Mustang over doing his homework. Considering he was likely the last surviving member of his graduating class, it had been a winning strategy — the only winning strategy. "You said the previous clue suggested Front House because the words 'far east' were written in lowercase letters to indicate a direction. Wouldn't the riddler have written 'this side of paradise' in uppercase letters case if he'd wanted us to think of a book's title?"

"Read enough books and you'll realize that most writers aren't as consistent as you as might think," Nathan replied.

"That right? Sounds like our riddle writer should've fired his editor."

Nathan offered John a perplexed look.

"Moving right along — let's see if we can find a copy of that book."

Nathan turned to the bookshelf and browsed through the hardcover volumes. John joined him, finding it difficult to read the titles embossed on the covers in the dim light. He took the lantern from the nightstand. Its wick held the flame of his first match. Light in hand, he resumed helping Nathan scan the shelves.

"Have you figured out how these books are sorted?" John asked.

"No, I don't see any rhyme or reason to it," Nathan replied.

With a grunt and a shake of his head, John continued to survey the titles, skimming his index finger across the bindings.

His finger stopped. He'd found the prize, a copy of *This Side of Paradise* by F. Scott Fitzgerald, sitting between *Ulysses* and *Main Street* on the lowest shelf. He pulled it out and examined its dust jacket, which bore the image of a man and woman in formal attire. John vaguely recalled the story — something about wealth and lost love, if he remembered correctly. The book had suffered heavy wear, with pages creased, dog-eared, and torn. Over a hundred years old, it was a genuine collector's item, yet on Mallard Island it was only one of many such treasures.

"Got it," John said.

"Oh? Great." From the tone of Nathan's voice, it was clear that he'd hoped he would find the book first.

"You want to open it?" John asked.

"How'd you guess?" Nathan eagerly snatched the book from John's extended hand and carefully began to page through it.

"Why don't you check the front and back covers, first?"

"Good idea." Nathan checked inside the front cover and then the back, before opening to the title page.

"Check this out! It's a signed copy." He held the book open for John to see. Lo and behold, F. Scott Fitzgerald's name was scrawled beneath the book's title in tall, narrow, scrawling black letters.

"I bet it would've been worth a fortune before the world fell to pieces. Unfortunately that doesn't help us now. Keep looking," John encouraged. He hoped they'd be able to unravel this note's secret as quickly as the last. As he watched Nathan flip through the pages, however, it soon became clear they would have no such luck.

"Nothing here," Nathan sighed, after thoroughly paging through the book several times.

"Let me have a look," John said, carefully taking the antique book from Nathan's hands. Save for a few red wine stains splotched across the inner pages, he found nothing. He handed the book back over to let Nathan.

A half hour later, they had discovered no further clues. Lightning flashed anew as the storm gained strength. Raindrops caught in the lightning's flare streamed wildly down the windowpanes. Thunder cracked violently, echoing and reechoing through the moist air that hung above the island.

"It's getting late," John said. "Let's make some dinner and call it a night."

With a reluctant nod, Nathan agreed. The two men made their way back along the slippery, puddle-laden path to the Wannigan.

John took charge of dinner. As he dug through their packs, he realized their food supplies had dwindled alarmingly. Still, he took the last of their fresh meat and cooked it in a pan over the propane stove.

"I'm surprised that old gas stove still works," Nathan said, sitting at the table.

"Propane doesn't go bad like gasoline does. As long as the tank it's stored in doesn't leak, you can use it for years and years. We're just lucky no one got to this supply before us."

John soon finished preparing the meal. Exhausted, he and Nathan ate in silence. After dinner, he uncorked a bottle of wine and filled two glasses. The red wine had survived the years without going sour, and before long John found himself refilling his glass. Nathan, on the other hand, took one sip, set his glass down, and let it languish on the table, just as he'd done with the whiskey the night before.

After John finished savoring his second drink, he and Nathan returned to Front House to settle in for the night. John brought along the bottle, just in case a nightcap was required.

The two men slept soundly through the storm, which had passed by the next morning. The new day's thick moist air and dew laden pine needles and grass were the only reminders of the previous night's theatrical violence.

It would be the first of many mornings spent on the island.

Chapter 19

IT WAS FRIDAY night. Emiko crept through the streets of Duluth, sticking to the shadows where streetlights didn't reach. The night air, heavy with condensation, hung over her like the steam from a hundred whistling tea kettles. She slipped through the heat silently, taking each step forward with care.

The other day she'd overheard her neighbors, Smitty and Leonard, discussing an upcoming recruitment meeting for the Restoration Army. Though she wasn't sure what the two men were trying to restore, she'd tasked herself with finding out what they were up to. She couldn't afford to miss this meeting.

The place where the men had said they'd gather was an abandoned pub, formerly known as Big Buck's Burgers. The hole-in-the-wall pub was separated from Duluth's lively main street by a couple blocks of restaurants, apartments, and offices, most long-since empty.

Emiko came to the block that housed Big Buck's and turned into an alley that led around back. Her top priority was to remain invisible, especially since Smitty and Leonard knew she worked at the Lakefront Inn. The situation would sour quickly if they found out she was spying on them.

After weaving through the alley and creeping past a pair of rusty metal dumpsters, she arrived at the back door of the pub. Pressing her ear to the wooden door, she could hear people talking inside. The meeting had already started, and she was missing it! She tried the doorknob. It was unlocked. As she inched the door open, the conversation inside became clearer.

"... brought you here today to discuss the misgivings you have with the present establishment, the Republic of

Minnesota, and what can be done about them." Smitty was speaking, which didn't surprise Emiko. He was a snake's tongue more eloquent than Leonard.

Emiko slowly pried the door open. It led into the pub's kitchen. Seeing that it was empty, Emiko let herself in — stealthily, of course. The kitchen was a cramped room, with an oven, a refrigerator, a sink, and rows of cupboards lining both the floor and the space above the counter. A freely swinging door with wide gaps above and below it led into the main room — the source of the voices.

Emiko crawled to the door and peered through the bottom gap. In the dim lamplight of the next room, she could make out Smitty, Leonard, and five other men. They were seated in a loose half-circle, with Smitty standing before them.

"First, a question for every man present: What has the Republic done for you?" Smitty asked. He waited for responses.

"Nothin' I couldn't do better myself," one man said as he spit, sending a gooey ball of saliva splattering on the floor.

"That ain't true," countered another man. He wore a black baseball cap with two thin yellow stripes streaking down the middle. "The Republic has helped stabilize things around these parts."

"Is that right?" Smitty asked.

"The people in the statehouse print money for us — money that's actually worth a damn — and they establish laws for us to live by," replied the black-hatted man.

"That's true," Smitty said. "But I didn't ask what the Republic was doing — I asked about what the Republic has done for you. How have they helped you in particular?"

"Good money and stability have helped me plenty," the black-capped man persisted.

There was a moment of silence, as the other men struggled to think of a suitable answer to Smitty's question. Eventually, the youngest of the group, a man about Nathan's age, offered his opinion.

"We accept that the government can't offer us much at present," the young man said. "The Republic is still trying to establish itself. Maybe a few years from now it'll be ready to help us, the citizens, in turn."

"A maybe is hardly a sure thing." Smitty shrugged. "Anything else?"

There was no reply. The man who'd spat crossed his arms and snickered. Looking at the group, Emiko guessed that all of the men were younger than thirty. It appeared Smitty and Leonard were targeting young men — angry young men like the ones who'd kidnapped her and held her hostage at Sawbill Lake. Emiko's brow and lips tightened at the thought.

"So, what I've heard so far is that benefits provided by the Republic are minimal at best, nonexistent at worst," Smitty said. "Now, let's turn the tables. What is the Republic taking from you?"

"Taking from us?" the black-hatted man said, surprised. "Why, nothing, of course."

"Ha, you know that's a red-faced lie," the spitting man snorted. "You and I both know those do-nothings in the statehouse are slapping taxes on everything they can think of."

"Is that why my beers at the Drunken Loon are so expensive?" Leonard said, finally joining the conversation. Though he wasn't as well-spoken as Smitty, Emiko saw how he might be good at making inroads with a certain crowd.

"They did start taxing beer and liquor just last month," the youngest man said. "But that's to be expected, isn't it? The old U.S. government used to tax things, too, according to my pops. He told me it's a necessary sacrifice, for the good of the people of Minnesota."

"And that's all well and good, if you're getting something for your taxes. But from what I can gather, the deal you men have at the moment is pretty raw."

"Raw as a heifer's ass, I reckon," the spitting man jeered.

"Are vague promises about freedom and lower taxes all you two fellas have to offer?" asked the black-hatted man.

"Not at all," Smitty said. "Look, if you were getting roads, oil, cars, and other real returns for your tax dollars, I'd say you were getting a pretty fair bargain. But as it stands, you're paying taxes, you're giving the Republic of Minnesota your labor, and you're not getting anything in return." He paused dramatically. "Men, your Republic is taking advantage of you, plain and simple."

"Cheer, cheer!" cried the spitting man.

"I disagree. I'd say the Republic is using us effectively, to build for the future," the youngest man cut in.

"You don't have to sacrifice the present to build for the future," Leonard said. He stood up from his seat in the half-circle, turning to address the men. "Any of you driven a car before?"

Three hands went up — those of the black-hatted man, the spitting man, and a tall man with an acute receding hairline who had not yet spoken.

"You can't tell me you don't miss it," Leonard said. "What kind of wheels did you boys have?"

"A '67 Mustang," said the spitting man.

"A late model Mazda," the balding man said.

The black-hatted man squirmed slightly in his chair, before finally replying, "My mom's burgundy Chrysler minivan."

The men all began to laugh, leaving Emiko to wonder what was so funny about driving a burgundy minivan. A car was a car, after all, right?

"At least it wasn't a Prius," Smitty offered, trying to calm the laughter. Once the chuckles had died out, the black-hatted man spoke again.

"Okay, but why all this talk of cars?" he asked. "No one has a car anymore, and they're not going to be making a comeback anytime soon."

"You sure about that?" Leonard replied, his lips turning up into a sly grin.

"Unless you can show me otherwise, yes," the black-hatted man said.

"Take a look outside, gentlemen." Smitty said, sweeping his arm toward the front entrance.

"You have an honest-to-goodness car? In working condition?" the youngest man asked, rising excitedly from his seat.

"Go look for yourself, son," Leonard said, leading the way toward the door. One by one, the men stood and filed toward the door, some clearly more excited to get a glimpse of the car than others.

Emiko retracted her head from the gap under the swinging door and sat, leaning back against a cupboard. Frankly, she didn't see what the fuss was all about. Cars were nice, but she, her family, and everyone else in Frontier View had gotten along fine without them for the last eight or nine-odd years. After the Desolation, her family had driven a car up from Minneapolis and used it occasionally over the months that followed while they settled in and built their home. Once they ran out of gas, however, they did without.

Unfortunately, there were a few matters discussed in the meeting that she hadn't completely understood. She knew a bit about government and taxes, but since Frontier View had neither of those things — at least not to her knowledge — she had little understanding of them. What she did know, was that Smitty and Leonard were trying to recruit more men. Having seen them harass her brother and Beard outside of that bar, she was certain that whatever plans they were cooking would have a bitter taste.

Emiko heard the front door open and shut — a signal that the men were returning from looking at the car. Footsteps clattered in the main room. The men were heading for the kitchen.

She had to hide.

Emiko fell to her knees and crawled hurriedly from the door. The footsteps grew closer. She quietly swung open the door of the cupboard beneath the sink. Luckily it held only a few bottles of cleaning supplies, leaving her plenty of space to hide. She scrunched into the cupboard and closed the door behind herself.

Outside her crawl space, she heard the kitchen door fling open, creaking with each back and forth swing until it finally came to a stop.

"What do you make of all this?" Emiko recognized the voice as the balding man's.

"The car seems legit. I'm just not exactly sure what they're trying to sell us on." It was a new voice, likely the fifth man's.

"They have a point though. The Republic of Minnesota hasn't been doing much for us."

"Maybe. But a lot of times you don't miss something until it's gone."

"Either way, I don't hear the men in the statehouse talking about getting cars back on the roads. Maybe these two guys have their heads in the right place."

"Their priorities are different, for sure. Whether they're in line with yours and mine remains to be seen. I heard they caused a bit of trouble at the Drunken Loon the other night. Sounded like some other guy instigated it, though. An out-of-towner, a guy with a scruffy beard."

"That so? A guy with the audacity to sport a beard is bound to be a troublemaker, I imagine. Anyhow, why don't we go take a seat and hear them out?"

"I don't see why not. Shall we head back?"

"Let's."

Emiko heard receding footsteps, followed by the creaks of the swinging door. She had the kitchen to herself again. She scampered out from under the sink and resumed her surveillance of the neighboring room.

"That's all we have for you today, men," Smitty announced. "If you're interested in bringing civilization back to the world, and creating a government that works for everyone, come by here again next weekend — same time, same place. My partner and I will be returning to central headquarters in a few days, but a local member of our organization will be here to tell you all you need to know about the Restoration Army."

"Any questions?" Leonard asked. None of the men raised their hands. "Well then, Smitty, let's get a move on. It was a pleasure to meet all of you." He and Smitty circled the room, shaking each man's hand.

"A pleasure indeed. If you have any questions, we'll be at the Lakefront Inn for a couple more days yet. Just ask for Smitty."

With that, Smitty and Leonard strutted across the room and out the door. After they'd left, the other men chatted amongst themselves.

"You really think they can get us all cars?" the youngest man asked.

"Who knows?" said the black-hatted man. "Seems like an awful big risk though, getting involved in a politically charged movement like this." He turned to the spitting man. "What do you think?"

"They're just as full of crap as any other salespeople I've ever heard, but their crap don't sound half-bad."

"Are you three going to come again next week?" the balding man asked. "Just to get a better idea of what's involved, of course."

"We'll see," the fifth man said with a shrug, as he went for the door. "Come on, it's late. Let's get out of here."

"We'd best take some time to think on it. We'll just have to wait and see who's here again next week," the black-hatted man said. "Anyhow, you boys can head out first. I'll snuff out the light."

The other four men quickly filed out the door without complaint. The black-hatted man dutifully extinguished the lamp in the corner, reuniting the room with the shadows it knew so well. The man hurried out the front door, leaving the bar as abandoned as he'd found it — or so he thought.

Emiko sat on the tile floor, leaning against the kitchen wall. Was this how the green-vested men attracted new recruits, by luring them with vehicles and promises of a more prosperous future? If only the five men tonight knew the truth, about the kidnappings and the violence, maybe they'd have more objections to Smitty and Leonard's proposal.

Confident that the men had all left, Emiko rose to her feet and exited via the back door. The two presenters had mentioned they'd be returning to their headquarters within the next few days. Where could their headquarters be? Who was in charge? And how many people had they already recruited? Emiko mulled over these questions and more as she retraced her steps to the Lakefront Inn, trudging through the humid night air.

Chapter 20

WITHIN THE windowless confines of the Restoration Army's comm room, morning, afternoon, and night ran together into a seamless stretch of gray. The clock on the wall provided the only evidence that time hadn't stopped entirely. The minute hand circumnavigated the clock's face as the hour hand crept ahead, and now it was 1630 hours, leaving Ramses' just thirty minutes until shift change and freedom from tedium. After his shift, he intended to go check on Thunder, the horse he'd been gifted while making his frantic return to HQ.

Today had been slow. He'd overheard just one transmission, a routine recruitment update from a pair of men in Duluth. Since then, he'd spent his afternoon with his feet kicked up on the table, reading a paperback copy of *White Fang*. Initially, he'd always tried to maintain proper military deportment while on duty, but eventually, realizing that no one could see his poor posture through audio-only radio equipment, he'd decided it was acceptable to spend his long, lonely days in the most comfortable manner possible — feet on table and book in hand.

His eyes drifted from the pages of his book back to the clock. In just twenty eight minutes, the next unlucky stiff would arrive to relieve him.

"HQ? Do you copy? It's Lieutenant Bogues," a voice crackled over the radio's speaker

Ramses yanked his feet from the table, sat up straight, and slipped the radio's headset over his ears.

"This is HQ. I copy you, Lieutenant."

"Could you patch me through to the General?"

"Did you try his private frequency?"

"Sure did. No luck."

"Understood. I'll see what I can do, sir."

After sending a hail to the General's office radio, which elicited no response, Ramses returned to the lieutenant.

"He's not available at the moment, Lieutenant. Is there anything you'd like me to pass on to him?"

"That gun-toting gal is getting close to Mallard Island, and I'm not sure what my next step should be."

"Roger that, sir. I'll inform the General as soon as I'm able to get a hold of him."

"What do you think I should do, radio boy?"

Ramses paused, caught off guard both by the question and the casual, insulting syntax.

"Radio boy?" Ramses frowned. "Me, sir?"

"You're the one operating the radios, aren't you?"

"Yes, but I don't believe I'm qualified to provide an answer to your inqu —"

"That's too bad, because I'm asking you anyway, son."

"Ahem," Ramses cleared his throat. "Well, alright then. What is the situation exactly, Lieutenant?"

"As far as I know, we're headed to an island. A small island. I have no troubles tracking her over land, but tailing her over water is gonna be tricky. The thing is, I don't know how she plans to get to the island. Hell, I'm not even sure how I'll get there, especially if I wanna be sneaky about it."

Ramses took a moment to think. An idea dawned upon him.

"Sir, how sure are you that she's heading for the island?"

"Pretty damn sure at this point. The General said she was heading there and she's given me no reason to think otherwise."

"Then my suggestion is to head her off before she gets to the island, sir. You don't need to follow. You can lead."

"And how do you reckon I do that, son?"

"Commandeer a boat, perhaps? Your dossier states that you know how to sail. I trust you'll think of something, sir"

"Is that all you got? You're about as helpful as a wagon with square wheels."

Ramses sighed. "That's why I'm the radio boy, sir. Is there anything else I can assist you with?"

"Not unless you can send me a pack of Marlboros," Bogues grumbled.

"I'm afraid not, Lieutenant. I wish you the best of luck."

"Roger that. Bogues, signing out."

Ramses set the radio headset back down on the table and leaned back in his chair. He hadn't expected to spend his time in the comm room issuing commands. His advice to Bogues had been sound, had it not? Still, he didn't feel that it was his place to offer suggestions, especially not to his superiors.

Ramses tapped his fingers on the table. The clock read 16:42. If nothing else, the conversation with Bogues had brought him a few minutes closer to the end of his shift.

Chapter 21

ARISTOTLE SAT ON the end of the wooden pier, gazing toward the east as the first hint of morning light smudged the horizon. A gentle breeze blew in from Rainy Lake, caressing her short locks of brown hair.

She was here, here in Fort Frances, or at least what remained of it. Once it had been the Canadian neighbor to International Falls, Minnesota. Now it was a ghost town, with streets fully of rusty cars and buildings with shattered windows and collapsing roofs.

The city brought to mind the Desolation. Each community had reacted differently to the event. The forsaken state of Fort Frances suggested that after the virus hit, the survivors — probably less than a hundred of them, judging from the size of the city — had conducted a frenzied exodus, leaving most everything behind. Had the evacuees found the haven they'd sought — a place to rebuild their lives, to overcome despair, and to regain their lost faith? Only the sun, the moon, and the sky could say for sure.

Unlike in Fort Frances, survivors in other cities had rallied together, using the tragedy as an opportunity for rebirth. Toronto was a prime example. The city's population had doubled in the decade following its post-Desolation crash. Even with that impressive rate of growth, however, the population was still a mere two-percent of what it had been prior to the apocalyptic catastrophe.

How long would it take for the world's population to again reach a billion, much less eight billion? It wouldn't happen within Aristotle's lifetime. That much was certain.

Before her, the hair-thin upper crescent of the great orange sun emerged from the far edge of the lake. Its light cast a glistening white pillar across the calm waters of Rainy Lake. All she had to do now was find a way to Mallard Island, a task that her deep-seated fear of open water made her dread.

Prior to the Desolation, when she'd been a primary school student, she'd lost her father to the frigid waters of Lake Superior. He and a friend had sailed out early on a clear morning in late September for a weekend excursion to Isle Royale. That afternoon Superior's notoriously unpredictable weather went rogue. Heavy rain and large hail pelted the lake. Gale force winds spawned fifty-foot waves. Her father's radio fell silent. His sailboat never returned to shore, and neither the bodies nor the remains of the boat were ever recovered.

Now, the looming expanse of Rainy Lake evoked the pain of those distant but still vivid memories. Despite losing her father, there was a part of him that still lived on in her. He'd bestowed her with immunity from the virus, a rare genetic gift.

When the sun had risen a few degrees above the placid waters of Rainy Lake, Aristotle pulled her legs up from the pier and stood tall. Sunrise would revisit the lake tomorrow, but the man she was after, John Osborne, would visit Mallard Island only once. She had no intention of missing her unscheduled appointment with him.

"Beautiful sunrise, ain't she?"

Aristotle spun around, startled by the gruff male voice. She reached for her holstered revolver, wrapping her fingers around the grip.

"Whoa, sister, I don't mean no trouble," said the man, raising his hands in the air.

Aristotle's hand didn't budge from the revolver's grip. The man remained still, clearly waiting for her to move first. He had a full head of graying hair, shaggy around the ears, with bangs hanging down to his eyebrows, and wore a loose green flannel shirt over a pair of ragged khakis. A narrow scar ran underneath his left eye — from a knife wound, perhaps. Most importantly, however, his hands were empty and he appeared to be otherwise unarmed.

Aristotle released the revolver and let her arm relax. "You can never be too careful," she said.

"Didn't mean to surprise you," the man said, lowering his arms. "I get a bit excited when I see a fellow soul is all. It ain't often I see real, living people around these parts."

Aristotle eyed the man warily. How had she let him sneak up on her? Had all the time she'd spent traveling through the forest alone dulled her senses? Luckily, this guy appeared to be innocuous.

"You from around here?" she asked, offering a smile to lighten the mood.

"Born and raised, but I left when I turned eighteen and just came back a year or two ago. Wanted to see if I could get by living on my own in these parts."

Aristotle nodded. The man's story was plausible enough.

"The name's Gallagher, by the way," the man said.

"My pleasure, Gallagher. You can call me Aristotle."

Gallagher chuckled. "You some kind of philosopher?"

Aristotle shook her head. "Just a nickname," she said. "So, you live here alone? How do you manage?"

"The usual." Gallagher pulled a hand-rolled cigarette and a lighter out of his shirt pocket. "You mind if I have a smoke? It's not tobacco, just an herbal mix I made myself. Doesn't ease my hankerin' for nicotine, but it's the next best thing."

"Go ahead," Aristotle said, peering at Gallagher's stainless steel Zippo lighter, engraved with a pair of uppercase letters. "What do the initials 'GB' stand for, by the way?"

"What, this?" Gallagher finished lighting his cigarette, then took a moment to examine the lighter. Beside the long wooden pier a hungry fish jumped, sending an expanding series of concentric rings rippling across the calm water.

"My brother gave me this Zippo a long time ago. 'GB' are my initials," Gallagher said. "This particular logo also represents a sports team. You ever hear of the Green Bay Packers?"

"I don't believe I have. Who were they?"

"The Packers were a team in the National Football League. They won more Super Bowls than any other team. The greatest champions."

"I see. I can recall the names of a few hockey teams — the Toronto Maple Leafs, the Winnipeg Jets — but that's where my sports knowledge ends."

"Sounds like you're Canadian."

"Yeah, you could say I'm Canadian. Not that where I was born matters much these days."

"Maybe, sister, but sometimes where you came from is just as important as where you're going," Gallagher said, flicking ash from his cigarette into the lake.

"What's your last name?" Aristotle asked, curious about what the 'B' stood for.

"Sorry, sister, but I usually don't give a gal my last name 'til after we get married," he replied with a wry smile.

Aristotle rolled her eyes. "Anyway, you were saying, about how you get by?" she said, circling back to the prior topic.

"Oh, right. This time of year I hunt deer and elk, or moose if I can find them. In the winter, I mostly stick to trapping. And, of course, I also go fishing from time to time, takin' my boat out on the lake and —"

"You have a boat?" Aristotle raised her eyebrows.

Gallagher took a drag of his cigarette. "Yeah, a big ol' sail boat. Used to take her out on Lake Superior. It's a shame she's confined to Rainy Lake these days."

Aristotle put a hand on her hip and looked out toward the rising sun, listening to the gentle lapping of the waves below. A steady breeze had sprung up. She needed to get to Mallard Island, but wasn't sure if she wanted to impose on this stranger — or trust his sailing ability. Still, if he was willing ...

She turned back to Gallagher. "You ever take passengers?"

"Usually not, but I'll make an exception for you, sister." Gallagher said, winking at her. Aristotle couldn't tell if the wink was a come-on or merely a playful gesture from the older man. Perhaps the answer lay somewhere in between.

"Where you headed?" Gallagher asked.

"Mallard Island. You know it?"

"Know it? Why, of course I know it." Gallagher blew smoke from his nose, before unceremoniously flicking his cigarette butt into the lake. "It's the most famous island on the whole damn lake."

"And what makes you say that?"

"Ernest Oberholtzer lived there, that's why. Protector of the great white north and conservation pioneer. A real man amongst men!"

"That's right." Aristotle agreed. "Glad to hear you know your history."

"You knew?" Gallagher furrowed his brow.

"Of course. I have a book about the island in my backpack." Aristotle reached back to pat the pack that hung from her shoulders.

"Oh? Where'd you manage to find that?"

"I borrowed it from the library."

Gallagher smiled slyly. "I bet the librarian didn't ask to see your library card."

"How'd you guess? Now, how about you show me this boat of yours?"

* * *

Aristotle followed Gallagher to a single story house near the lake. Judging from its exterior, the modest home hadn't seen a paintbrush, a putty knife, or a caulking gun since the Desolation. A missing panel of siding revealed the brick and mortar foundation underneath.

"You live here?" Aristotle asked.

"Nah, just dock my boat here," Gallagher replied.

They circled behind the house. A swath of overgrown yard separated them from the lake. After wading through the waist-high weeds, they arrived at a narrow dock made of wooden planks.

"There she is," Gallagher said, proudly sweeping his arm toward the sailboat. The craft was much smaller than Gallagher's description had led her to expect, perhaps suitable for a family of four. The boat's name, "Viking Vixen," was affixed to the white fiberglass hull in purple lettering. Its mast was rigged with a rainbow-striped sail.

Aristotle stepped to the edge of the dock to inspect the boat. It had a two padded benches for passengers. At the base of the mast was a storage compartment, almost like a miniature cabin. The space was sufficient for storing gear, but too tight for a person to squeeze into, save perhaps for a small child.

"May I?" she asked, placing one foot in the craft.

"Of course. She ain't gonna sink," Gallagher said with a chuckle. "You afraid she's not seaworthy?"

"Just making sure there aren't any rats on board," Aristotle joked, half-seriously. Though her fear of water gave her pause, she cautiously stepped into the boat one leg at a time. The craft rocked slightly under her weight, but quickly stabilized.

The boat bobbed gently as Gallagher hoisted himself in. After securing his footing, he opened the storage compartment.

"I have my shotgun in here. Hope that don't bother you none."

"I don't think I have the moral authority to object," Aristotle said, patting her holstered pistol. She noted that Gallagher also had a radio and a backpack in the compartment. "Mind if I put my gear in there?"

Gallagher grinned. "Go right on ahead, sister."

As she stowed her pack in the compartment, Aristotle took a close look at Gallagher's firearm, a Benelli M4. The sleek, black combat shotgun possessed ample power to take down any Northwoods beast without trouble, bull moose included. Though she was unsure why Gallagher possessed such a powerful weapon, Aristotle's experiences had taught her that, in the disarray of the post-Desolation world, too much firepower was better than too little. Gallagher clearly shared her sentiment.

"You ready to sail?" Gallagher asked.

"Yeah, I'm set." Aristotle closed the storage compartment. "Will you need any help?"

"Nah. This rig is easy enough for one person to handle."

It was just as well. Aristotle had never manned a sailboat. Furthermore, she wasn't sure how her body and spirit would react to the ride on the open lake. She took a seat on the cushioned bench.

Gallagher knelt down to untie the two ropes that secured the sailboat to the dock. He then adjusted the sail, setting course across the shimmering blue expanse toward the rapidly rising sun and Mallard Island.

Chapter 22

MALLARD ISLAND had once been a beacon of hope. This tiny island was so narrow that John could throw a stone across even its widest point, so short that he could walk from end to end in five minutes. This island, with so many books strewn about its ten buildings that it would take twenty lifetimes to read them all, was supposed to have provided him with answers.

Four days after their arrival, those answers weren't forthcoming.

Unable to find anything of use within *This Side of Paradise,* John and Nathan had spent the second day scouring the island for more clues, discovering none. In the meantime, they'd learned quite a bit about Ernest Oberholtzer, the island's longtime inhabitant. Ober, as he'd been called, had spent his life defending the sanctity of the wilderness and protecting the north from the encroachment of industry. In his later years, he'd seldom left Mallard Island, spending the twilight of his life with his books in hermitic fashion.

After Ober's death in 1977, a group of volunteers had formed a non-profit foundation to preserve his island and his legacy. The foundation had actively pursued its mission until the early 2020s. According to the logbook, visits to the island had dwindled through the first half of the decade before stopping altogether in 2025. These records confirmed what Victor had said, while still leaving John and Nathan to wonder what had caused the visitations to cease two years before the Desolation.

On the morning of the third day, John had split the last of their venison jerky and pilot biscuit rations with Nathan. They'd spent that day becoming intimately familiar with the signed Fitzgerald hardcover, Nathan rereading it and John finally atoning for his failure to read it in high school. A thorough reading of the book again yielded nothing. Worse yet, that third evening they'd gone without dinner, unable to find any game on the island and unwilling to open the rusty cans of food stacked in the back corner of the Wannigan.

All through that night and into the morning of the fourth day, John's stomach growled with hunger. Mallard Island had become their island prison, their Alcatraz. Their canoe was sunk, they'd run out of food, and if their situation didn't improve, John knew his weakening body wouldn't sustain him much longer.

John sat at the long table in the lower level of the Wannigan, nursing his second glass of red wine. Wine wasn't typical breakfast fare for John, but he figured any calories were better than no calories. Nathan sat opposite him, elbows on the table and head resting on his hands. The notebook containing the clues lay open beside him.

John's strength was fading fast. Though he'd punched new hole in his belt, he could already feel his jeans riding loosely on his hips. Ordinarily, the lack of food would cause his metabolism to slow down, but now something was steadily consuming his muscle and fat stores. That "something" was likely his arm.

He raised the half-empty bottle of Merlot and filled his glass a third time. He swirled the wine, savored the bouquet, and took a long sip. The wine was a pleasant, mind-numbing diversion, but it didn't alter the hard fact that he was out of options. He was weak, tired, irritable, and growing resigned to his impending fate.

"We could try some of the canned goods," Nathan suggested. He stared at the wall, avoiding eye contact with John.

"Have you looked at the cans? Some are bulging seriously. Even the best preserved canned goods go bad after a couple years," John said. "But if you wanna give yourself a case of botulism, go right ahead."

"How about fishing?"

"Haven't seen a rod and reel anywhere, not to mention fishing line," John replied.

Nathan idly tapped his fingers on the table. "How about getting off the island? We could try to get this boat floating again." Examination in the light of day had revealed that Wannigan was not an ordinary building but in fact a kitchen boat, which Ober had brought ashore and winched from the water to serve as the island's main office and dining room.

"No chance. It's been exposed to the elements all these years — I'm sure the hull is full of leaks. Best she remains grounded."

Nathan's fingers stopped dancing on the table. He eyed John.

"We could swim back. I bet we could find some life jackets lying around somewhere," he said.

John shook his head. "Maybe we could swim to one of the adjacent islands, but it's a long way back to shore and I don't think we'd make it. Besides, the water's damn cold." He paused to think. Even if they did make it back to shore, what would he do? No matter how much he ate, he continued to lose weight. He didn't know for sure that Mallard Island had the answers he sought, but he saw no alternative. "We came here looking for something. We're not gonna leave until we find it."

"You don't seem to be looking very hard right now," Nathan replied, his frustration evident.

"We're out of leads."

"Then maybe we should go hunt for some."

"Maybe," John said, taking another sip of wine.

Nathan stood up, pounding his palms on the edge of the table. It was an aggressive display that, coming from Nathan, caught John off guard.

"Look, John — I know there's something you're not telling me. I'm not blind. I can see you're losing weight. I saw you fixing your belt. If you have a problem, why the hell don't you let me know? Maybe we can tackle it together."

"Maybe this one is beyond fixing," John said. Though his health — maybe even his life — lay on the line, he was out of ideas. Death by starvation would be unpleasant, but, with no family left, at least he would leave no one behind.

Nathan glared at him, long and hard. "'Never quit. Never quit, no matter how long the odds are.' Do you know who said that to me?"

John shrugged.

Nathan let out a deep sigh of frustration and shook his head. He grabbed his notebook and stormed towards John. Snatching the still nearly-full glass of wine from the table, he raised it to his lips and chugged it down.

"Nathan, what are you doing?" John asked, unimpressed.

Nathan slammed the glass down on the table. John was surprised it didn't shatter.

"I can't stand just sitting here, watching you drink," he said, making a frown of repulsion. "How can you enjoy that mashed-grape death juice? And for breakfast, no less."

"It grows on you," John said.

Nathan glared at John. "I'm gonna go outside and look for answers. I'd love it if you'd join me. And if it wouldn't be too much trouble, I'd appreciate it if you'd let me know what the Desolation is going on with you, because I can't believe you would drag me all the way out here only to keep me half in the dark." With that, he stomped up the short flight of stairs and barged out the door, letting it slam behind him.

John rested his elbows on the table, staring at the unopened bottles of wine along the wall. Though tempted, he knew his empty stomach wouldn't deal well with more alcohol. Best to quit now.

He'd give the kid a few minutes to blow off his head of steam, then go deliver the grim news — that he suspected the bionic arm was leeching away his life force. He wasn't sure how Nathan would take the news, but he deserved to know.

He also deserves a partner that doesn't give up, John thought. The kid had already lost his father a year earlier, while on a similar journey in search of help. John wanted no part in reenacting that experience.

* * *

Nathan couldn't deny the obvious truth: John was losing weight and vigor, fast. Though John's mind was a tightly closed book, after spending weeks with the laconic man a silent rapport had developed between them. Clearly, something was terribly wrong with John. More troubling, though, was that John had lost hope that a remedy could be found.

Nathan hung his head as he wandered along the shoreline. Waves lapped calmly against the rocky shore, creating a soft, rhythmic backbeat to accompany a house wren practicing his trill. At the island's edge, Nathan spotted their canoe, fifteen feet from shore, peacefully resting just beneath the lake's surface. He considered wading across the sharp rocks to retrieve it, but the severely crumpled and jaggedly torn hull told him it was beyond salvaging.

Nathan could feel his cheeks growing warm. An effect of the wine, perhaps? He recalled that his father's face would flush after a single beer. He wished he hadn't bolted the glass down. Right now, it was important that he think clearly. He reached down, filling his cupped hands with cool water and splashing it on his face.

He stepped back from the shore. He wanted to do something to help John; staring at the crippled canoe didn't qualify. In his mind, Nathan replayed the conversation they'd just had. John had rejected all suggestions for leaving the island. Clearly, escape wasn't John's goal.

The key to unlocking John's arm was here on Mallard Island, somewhere, waiting to be found, if only they could decipher the clues that the riddler had left. In that effort, Nathan was failing miserably. Was John disappointed that he'd been unable to crack the second riddle? Nathan imagined himself the clever sidekick, the partner who provided the occasional flash of insight to John, the world-savvy action hero. Even in that limited capacity Nathan had only served to disappoint.

This was his last chance. The solution was here. Nathan had to figure out what the riddler meant. He had to do it now.

"Hmm ..." He pursed his lips in thought, pulling his handwritten copy of the clues from the pocket of his jeans and carefully analyzing the lines. The riddles were short, wasting not a single word ...

His eyes grew wide. *Beyond this side of paradise.* Beyond! The solution was so blindingly obvious. How had he not thought of it earlier?

At once, he dashed toward Winter House, throwing the door open and returning to the bookshelf beside the fireplace. Falling to one knee, he quickly located the empty gap where John had found *This Side of Paradise.* Moving past the vacant space, he selected the next book in line and yanked it from the shelf.

Nathan stared at the hardcover in his hands. The book was *Main Street,* written by Sinclair Lewis, an author with whom he wasn't familiar. The thick volume had long since lost its dust jacket and the corners of its navy blue binding were worn with age. Nathan carefully flipped open the cover and turned to the title page. There, affixed beneath the title, he discovered a yellow post-it.

"Loons over the moon!" he exclaimed. He took the pencil from his pocket and furiously copied the clue into his notebook. He then returned the book to its place along the shelf and ran from Winter House to deliver the good news to John.

As he neared the Wannigan, he stopped short and furtively examined the scene. On the opposite side of the island he spied a sailboat, tethered to the wooden dock. It surely hadn't been there when he'd stepped out from the Wannigan.

Someone else had come to the island, but who? More importantly, why?

Nathan found the widest tree he could, a densely branched spruce, and hid behind it, trying to observe the boat without being seen. He clutched the notebook tightly to his chest.

Standing near the dock was a person, wearing a loud crimson top that clashed with the natural surroundings like a white-as-snow polar bear picnicking with a party of brown grizzlies. The figure, his back to Nathan, stared out into the vastness of Rainy Lake. He wore blue jeans and had short brown hair. As Nathan continued to watch he realized that the object of his vigil wasn't a he, but rather a she.

Nathan ducked back behind the spruce tree. He was feeling light-headed from the wine. He closed his eyes and shook his head.

Why had this woman — it was definitely a woman, Nathan decided — come to Mallard Island? Was she seeking the same thing as he and John?

Nathan glanced at the notebook in his hand, rereading the clue to himself:

The sun sets here
on the furthest shore
but where the sun rises
push down on the floor

The meaning was simple enough, he thought. Hopefully this clue would be the last, and he and John would soon be able to unravel the mystery of John's arm and then focus on finding a way off the island.

Nathan turned to run to the Wannigan. He had to share the new clue with John and alert him of the arrival of the sailboat. Before setting out, he looked back over his shoulder at the stranger by the dock. The woman was still facing the lake. The Wannigan wasn't far.

Staying behind trees as much as possible to avoid drawing the woman's attention, Nathan hurried back. As he darted from one tree to the cover of the next, however, he discovered another man already there. Before Nathan could react, the man swung a dark object at his forehead and the world went black.

Chapter 23

THE MYSTICAL allure of the lake in the morning sun continued to beg for her attention, yet eventually Aristotle had to pull away. It was time to find John Osborne, if indeed he was on the island, and determine what role he was playing in the restlessness that was brewing in the north.

Gallagher had gone ahead, venturing off to explore the island on his own and leaving Aristotle to do likewise. Though she'd thought it a poor idea, she didn't feel she had the authority to order the older man around. Besides, in truth she relished the solitude afforded by his absence, leaving her to enjoy the gossiping birds and the playful lapping of the waves against the shore.

Meandering inland, Aristotle could see a few buildings. The nearest was a small white house, which appeared to be a converted boat. Farther in the distance, to both the east and west, she could see wooden, two-story buildings. If other structures existed on the island, they were obscured by the trees.

She cautiously approached the white houseboat, trying not to look conspicuous. If she encountered anyone, she hoped to do so cordially. She didn't want it to appear that she was snooping around — never mind that she was doing just that.

Not far from the houseboat she spotted a small white object, apparently litter, lying on the ground beside a tree. Closer examination revealed it to be a spiral-bound notebook with its cover folded back. Picking it up, she could see that it hadn't been outside for long. Though a few streaks of dirt marked its pages, the notebook bore no signs of having recently been exposed to the elements. Considering the storms that had passed through just days earlier, it must have been dropped recently. Someone was on the island now, or had been within the last couple days.

On the open page of the notebook were a handful of phrases, scrawled in pencil — poems, perhaps, with meanings that weren't immediately clear.

As she tried to decipher the lines, the tall, dark shadow of a man approached, taking a place beside her own. The stranger's shadow came complete with voice.

"I'd recognize that red hoodie and that massive revolver anywhere. Never expected I'd see them out here."

It was him. John Osborne. Aristotle remained still, standing stiff as the subzero air on a windless winter night.

"Hands in the air. Turn around slowly," Osborne said. Aristotle complied, raising both hands and rotating to face her captor.

Osborne's pistol arm was extended, leveling his iconic, long-barrel Colt .45 at her. He looked much the same as he had the day they'd first met a few months ago in Franco's Saloon. The scruffy beard still covered his chin and cheeks. Notably, however, Osborne had lost a striking amount of weight. Though he hadn't been a burly man before, now he was downright anorexic.

"What are you doing here, Aristotle?" he asked, spitting out her name with a trace of contempt.

"I was looking for you, in fact," Aristotle replied, trying to project an air of calm.

"How'd you know to find me here?"

"Rumors. Hearsay. As you likely know, Osborne, things are changing in in the north. I wanted to find out what role you're playing in those changes."

Aristotle tried to get a read on Osborne, but whether he knew something about the General or nothing at all, his expression gave no indication. What she saw before her was a man exhausted. Osborne looked like he was having trouble holding it together.

"Where'd you get that notebook?" Osborne asked.

"I found it on the ground, right here."

Osborne paused to contemplate her words.

"Have any way to prove that?"

"I'm afraid not." Aristotle shook her head. "Is it yours?"

"Look, I don't have time or patience for games. If I find out you did anything to the owner of that notebook, I'll shoot you where you stand."

"You're not the owner, then?"

"You're not in a position to be asking questions," John retorted. "You come here to shoot me?"

"No," Aristotle said. The question seemed absurd, though she supposed their previous encounter warranted it. "You've done nothing to incur my wrath, at least not as far as I'm aware."

"How considerate of you," John muttered. "Are you here alone?"

"I came with a man, in his sailboat." Aristotle nodded in the direction of the boat. "But it seems I've lost track of him."

"He's not the only person who's gone missing," John said, shaking his head and exhaling deeply. "You're really not here to make good on your threat?"

"For the last time, no!" Aristotle exclaimed.

"Can you blame me? You had a gun on me last time we met."

"Different time, different circumstances. "

John remained silent as he considered her exasperated assertion. The pistol remained pointed at her like a rattlesnake ready to strike, until finally he lowered his gun arm.

"If I see you reach for your weapon, you know what'll happen," he said.

"Understood." Aristotle nodded.

"I hope I don't regret this." John holstered his Colt. "Lower your arms and hand me that notebook."

Aristotle handed him the notebook. John looked at the open page.

"Well, I'll be. He figured it out," John mumbled, rubbing his beard.

"Who figured what out?"

"My partner, he cracked the next clue." John shot Aristotle a piercing gaze. "You swear you haven't seen him? Seventeen, kind of scrawny, black hair and tan skin." He gestured with his free hand, approximating his partner's height.

Aristotle shook her head. "You're the first person I've encountered on this island, Osborne."

"You said you came here with a man?"

"Whom I haven't seen since we arrived, fifteen or twenty minutes ago."

"Then be on your guard. We might have unfriendly company. My partner and I came here knowing we might be stepping into a trap." John closed his eyes, taking a deep breath.

"You doing alright?" Aristotle asked.

"Do you have any food?"

"Do you always answer questions with another question?"

John responded with a cold, tired glare.

"Point taken," Aristotle said. "Yeah, I have food. From the smell of your breath, I'm guessing you had beer for breakfast."

"Wine. Red wine. We ran out of food."

Aristotle pointed to the houseboat. "You came from that building?"

"Yeah. The Wannigan."

"Interesting name. Let me get some food from my pack and then meet you in there. Who knows, maybe our missing persons are waiting for us inside."

"I wouldn't count on it," John said, holding up the notebook in his hand. "I know Nathan. He wouldn't leave this behind."

* * *

Nothing made sense.

John sat at the table, his still empty glass of breakfast wine and the notebook before him. His unexpected encounter with Aristotle had brought home to him the severity of his weakness. As much as he wanted to search for Nathan immediately, he knew he'd be worthless without eating first.

The abandoned notebook made it clear that something had happened to Nathan. The kid wouldn't have carelessly tossed it aside. Someone must have snatched him, but who? And why did they take Aristotle's partner as well?

It troubled John that he had no way to verify Aristotle's story. Maybe she didn't have a partner at all. Maybe she'd even disposed of Nathan herself. Still, she seemed honorable, and John felt inclined to trust her ... which wasn't to say he wouldn't keep a close eye on her.

It also wasn't clear why she'd come looking for him. She seemed to think he was involved in changes that were occurring in the north. If John was somehow wrapped up in a larger plot — certainly a possibility, given the glut of dubious characters with whom he'd recently crossed paths — he was unaware of his own involvement.

He pushed the thought aside. For now his priorities were to feed his starving body and then go find Nathan. So long as Aristotle was cooperative, analyzing her intentions could wait.

John heard the door open and shut. Aristotle appeared in the stairwell.

"Help yourself to the wine. The Shiraz is good," John offered.

"I'll pass, thanks." Aristotle set a cloth sack on the table. "I brought a little ham and some rye bread. Will it be enough?"

"Yeah, it'll do." John took out a few slices of ham and rye to make a sandwich.

Aristotle sat across from him. "Can I see the notebook again?"

"Sure," John said, sliding it across the table. She examined the page.

"You said these are clues?"

John nodded, taking a bite from his sandwich. "We found the first clue here in the Wannigan. It led to the second clue. That one gave us some trouble, but apparently Nathan finally worked out its meaning before he *conveniently* disappeared," he said.

Aristotle rolled her eyes. "I told you, I haven't seen your partner."

John shrugged.

Aristotle continued. "I came here because one of the General's men told me I could find you here."

"The General?" John asked.

"My source said you were working for the General as well."

"Well, your source was wrong. It's been years since I've dealt with any generals, and I'd like to keep it that way." John finished his sandwich, and opened the sack to make another. "I'd make an exception for General Mills, though."

Aristotle was unamused. "So, where do we look first? After you finish stuffing your face, of course."

John frowned. "We could start by scouring the island."

"Any chance the clue will help us? Maybe your partner — Nathan, you said, right? — already figured it out."

"It's a possibility, but solving these riddles takes time and I'm not sure we have time to waste."

"Says the man lounging around and eating his second sandwich."

John shook his head. Just ten minutes with fresh company and already he missed Nathan.

Aristotle stood up from the table and walked over to the map that hung on the wall.

"This is a map of the island, right?"

"Right," John uttered indistinctly through a mouthful of sandwich.

"The clue says 'The sun sets here on the furthest shore.' That's probably this building on the western tip, Japanese House." Aristotle pointed to the map.

John finished the sandwich and licked his fingers clean. "I suppose we can start there."

* * *

The crystal clear sky and bright sun of early afternoon bore down as Aristotle and John approached Japanese house. Though the building's design conveyed a Far Eastern aesthetic, its heavy-duty hardwood construction and a wiry outer mosquito net were pure Minnesota. The netting served to remind Aristotle that she was in the Northwoods and not in Edo period Japan. Still, the open air design and lake front location would've likely made it one of Ober's favored places to pass the dog days of summer.

"You ever been to Japan?" Aristotle asked.

"Unfortunately, no." John shook his head. "By the time I enlisted, the U.S. didn't have much say in that part of the world."

"A passport still would've gotten you in."

"And sky high airfare would've kept me out. I went where the Marines wanted me to go and that was it. Didn't see much reason to spend a fortune on some extravagant vacation. Near the end, civilian airfare from New York to Tokyo would've run me a couple months' worth of salary."

"Better than any deal you'll find now," Aristotle said.

John didn't reply, as the awkward companions continued down the rocky trail that led to the entrance of Japanese House.

He seems different, somehow, Aristotle thought. Witnessing John's obvious concern for his missing partner showed her another side of the man, one that went beyond the devil-may-care attitude he'd displayed during their first encounter. Even then, during their previous meeting, she'd immediately sensed that he knew how to handle himself. What she saw now was that he was able to care for others, too. It was a trait that, in these desperate times, not all men still possessed.

"You know, Osborne, I came here to find you, but I'm still not exactly clear on what you're doing here."

"Everything revolves around this." John raised his left arm, the one that she'd seen hurl a man across the length of a saloon. "Come on, let's go in." He opened the screen door to Japanese House.

Aristotle followed, stepping into the screened-in porch, which was built around a single interior room. Together the porch and the surrounding room looked like two squares, the smaller one enclosed within the larger one. She circled around the perimeter of the porch, stopping on the far side to gaze out at the placid blue lake and lush green islands to the west. After admiring the view, she turned and passed through the double wooden doors that led into the interior room. Already John was inside, having come in through the opposite door.

The room itself was barren, suitable only for meditation or perhaps for study. On the floorboards were four Japanese characters, painted by hand in a once vibrant red that had faded over the years.

"You read Chinese?" John asked her.

"No, but the meaning is clear. Each character represents one of the cardinal directions — north, south, east, west." She knelt by the one that she presumed meant "east," the location of the rising sun, and pushed down against the floorboards. Her effort elicited no response.

"Don't you mean Japanese, by the way?" she asked.

"They're one and the same, for the most part," John said. "Japan borrowed most of their writing system from China. Not that I can read either language."

"Oh? I didn't know," Aristotle said, again pushing on the floorboards to no avail. "Anyway, I thought pushing down here, 'where the sun rises,' would do the trick ..." she said, returning to her feet. "Though if it were that easy, I suppose someone else would've activated it by now."

"Maybe you just gotta push harder," John said, taking a knee. "Let me try."

Aristotle stepped back and stood in the middle of the small room, watching. Even after his meal, John still looked haggard. He was clearly running on fumes. Aristotle doubted that he'd be able to accomplish what she hadn't been able to. Then again, creatures fighting for survival had been known to surprise.

"Are you seeing this?" John called for her attention. "My hand!"

Aristotle looked at the floor underneath the red Chinese character. An aura of pure white had coalesced around John's left hand, causing his fingers to glow with a shimmering radiance. Tiny white specks appeared on the back of his hand, dancing to and fro. Soon the specks multiplied, forming a stream of iridescent plasma that ran up his arm before disappearing under the sleeve of his shirt.

"What the Desolation is that?" Aristotle exclaimed. "Does it hurt?"

"I don't feel anything unusual," John said, his voice both excited and exhausted.

A loud rumble sounded from underfoot — a deep mechanical groan. The floorboards shifted beneath Aristotle's feet. She lost her footing and fell backward, expecting to crash onto the floor. Instead, she found herself free falling, tumbling down a bottomless black hole.

Chapter 24

JOHN'S ARM STOPPED glowing. He inched toward where Aristotle had stood.

"You hear me?" he called down the dark hole. A section of wooden floorboards had risen two inches and then, along a centerline, sprung apart into two retracting panels, exposing a hole in the middle of the room. Inside the hole was a metal slide, like a laundry chute crafted of construction grade steel, leading to depths unknown.

No response.

"You okay? I'd rather not deal with any more missing persons today," he shouted.

A loud click echoed from the darkness below, followed by a low humming sound that slowly grew louder.

"Then you're in luck," Aristotle's voice called. A moment later, John saw her familiar bright hoodie, seemingly levitating up the narrow corridor.

"Luck is hardly the word I'd use," John muttered. Aristotle's ascent stopped at ground level. Beneath her feet was a flat platform, about the size of an office desk, with a black gunmetal control panel in one corner. Though John had seen similar contraptions before, it was patently strange to see such a high tech device on this quiet wilderness island. The answers he sought were surely near.

"How long was the fall?" John asked.

"Long. But near the bottom some kind of safety net caught me, before breaking away and setting me down on this elevator platform."

John rubbed his beard, staring at the metal platform. "You'd think they'd just keep the elevator up here at ground level."

Aristotle shrugged. "Don't look at me. I didn't design the place." She pointed at the control panel. "Going down?"

"Let's," John said, joining Aristotle on the small platform. She flipped a small red switch. The elevator shook gently and descended, emitting a low hum. The sunlight steadily waned until the dim red glow of the control panel's switch was the only light that remained. John could see nothing in the darkness, not even his hands.

"You put on quite a light show a minute ago. How about an encore?" Aristotle asked.

"Don't ask me. Ask my arm."

Aristotle paused, hesitating. "I see. What's the story behind your arm, anyhow?"

"That's what I'm hoping to find out." John was also hoping to find Nathan. Although his gut feeling was that Nathan hadn't stumbled into this hole, his instincts told him that Nathan's disappearance and the hole were somehow connected. At any rate, now wasn't the time to turn back. Nathan had demonstrated that he could handle himself. No matter what had become of him, John was confident that the kid could fend for himself.

John's knees buckled as the ride ended with a sudden jerk.

"We're here," John announced. A chill ran down his spine as he recalled the hospital in which he'd woken up, a couple years prior. Though he could see nothing, the dead, stagnant air and the dull echo of his voice against the metal walls told him plenty about his environment.

"It sure looks that way," Aristotle replied. "Not that there's much to see."

John fumbled forward with one arm. Nothing but empty darkness.

"Got a light?" he asked.

"No, I don't smoke."

"So you start your campfires by rubbing two sticks together, like a good little girl scout?"

"I could ask the same of you, you know. How about we go back up and get a lantern?"

As though responding to Aristotle's suggestion, a single light came on overhead with a low-pitched shudder. It spread down in a cone like a lone spotlight on a stage. The first light was followed by another and another, each illuminating a section of the hallway ahead. At last the final light switched on, revealing a heavy blast door at the end of the corridor.

The walls flickered. John covered his eyes as halogen rays burst from the walls, banishing all shadows from the hallway with unfiltered white light.

"Power at twenty-five percent of operational capacity," a robotic voice droned. *"Lighting systems, fully active. Informational systems, fully active. Life-support systems, attempting reset. Security systems ..."*

"They're rolling out the digital red carpet for us," Aristotle said, speaking over the monotone of the computerized announcement.

"They've been waiting a long time. Sounds like it'll take a few minutes for all the systems to come online."

Aristotle glanced up at the lights. "Where does all the power come from?"

"Hard to say. I met a local who said the U.S. Navy had a strong presence on this lake in the final years before the Desolation. I have to imagine the Navy would've of known about the existence a facility like this, sitting right under their noses, so maybe they played a hand in supplying power. Could be solar, hydroelectric, or nuclear."

"Nuclear power here?"

"I wouldn't put anything past the Pentagon," John said, giving his left forearm a gentle rub.

"Hello, possessor of spear," the robotic voice greeted. *"Please step ahead, through the corridor."*

John raised an eyebrow. "Spear?"

"It sounds like the same voice my mom's iPhone had."

"I was more of an Android guy." John gestured down the corridor. "Shall we?"

"Ladies first," Aristotle mocked.

"Very funny," John grumbled, starting toward the door at the end of the long hallway. He dragged his fingers along the shining white walls as he passed, feeling the heat from the halogen bulbs that lay behind thin sheets of glass. As he arrived at the door the robotic voice droned from above.

"Please place the spear's palm on the access panel."

John examined the wide steel door. A gray touchscreen panel rested in the spot where a doorknob would typically protrude.

"Let me guess ..." John said as he spread his fingers apart and extended his hand towards the panel.

* * *

Nathan's weary eyelids struggled open. His head hurt like he'd been kicked by an angry tvapa. He tried to rub his forehead, only to find that his wrists were bound together behind his back.

Where am I? Craning his neck around, he saw that he was in Front House, where he and John had been spending their nights. He was lying on the floor, near the piano in the smaller room. His ankles had been tightly wrapped together with duct tape.

He couldn't recall how he'd arrived here. What could he recall, then? He'd left the Wannigan and discovered the next clue — a clue which he believed led to Japanese House. Then, he'd begun hurrying back to John ...

Outside, he heard the recriminations of an enraged man. The image of a shotgun stock bashing against his forehead rushed back into his memory. Was the man outside the same one who'd clobbered him? Nathan listened, hoping to find out.

"Why the hell didn't you tell me this was about John Osborne? You expect me to go toe-to-toe with him and his billion dollar arm?" The voice was one Nathan didn't recognize. He wondered if the man was working together with the woman he'd seen near the boat.

"You're a cocksucking lout for not telling me what you were sending me into. Ain't no way to treat a man, much less one of your own."

The man gradually began to calm down. Nathan realized he was hearing only one side of the conversation. Perhaps the man was speaking into a radio?

"Alright," the man's voice said. "So, you think Osborne holds the key to finding this Northland Core and you want me to pump him for the lowdown about it?"

The Northland Core? The name sounded vaguely familiar to Nathan, like something he'd read of, perhaps, many years ago.

"Yeah, he and that gal are underground now. Shouldn't be a problem to ambush them when they pop up topside. I got another trick up my sleeve, too, if it comes to that."

Nathan gulped. He had a bad feeling he was set to play a leading role in this man's game plan. His eyes darted frantically around the room, seeking a way to escape. He saw the piano, the piano bench, stacks full of music scores, a few paintings on the walls, a couple of empty plant pots, a half-full bottle of John's wine, a shotgun resting against a chair in the corner ...

"Got it. I'll report back to you once everything's taken care of, one way or the other."

The voice went silent. Nathan continued to listen carefully. He heard the man grumbling outside, cursing to himself. Shortly, the front door of the house creaked open. Nathan shut his eyes, pretending he was still out cold.

Footsteps echoed through the quiet interior, across the larger entry room and into Nathan's room, eventually stopping beside his head. Even with his eyes closed, Nathan could feel the man looming over him, could smell the stale smokiness of his breath.

"I'll leave you here for now," the man muttered. "No reason to show my hand before I gotta."

The man stood and continued across the room, before stopping in his tracks.

"Bastard thinks he's some kinda hot shot now that he's in charge of an army," the man chuckled, clearly amused. Nathan heard the scraping of a chair.

"But Osborne has seen better days. Maybe I stand a chance," the man snickered as he walked back across the small room and into the main room. The front door slammed shut a moment later.

When Nathan opened his eyes, the shotgun that had been resting against the chair was gone.

He had to escape. He had to warn John. But how?

Chapter 25

JOHN'S PALM RESTED on the door's digital hand reader.

"*Confirming serial number,*" the robotic voice announced. Again specks of light spread across John's palm and forearm as they had when he'd touched the floor, topside. A moment later the dots of light vanished and the monotone voice returned.

"*Serial number, zero zero zero one, confirmed. Please proceed. The creator awaits your arrival.*"

The door before them slowly rose, the rumble of churning gears reverberating throughout the narrow hallway.

"The creator?" Aristotle said with mild amusement.

"Probably some guy with a god complex."

"You know, some thinkers believed that scientists only wanted religion dead so that they could rise up and become gods themselves."

"We know how well that worked out. All gods, old and new, were powerless in the face of the Desolation."

"I take it you're not a believer."

"I believe in life and death. I don't worry about what comes before or after. You?"

"To be honest, I'm not sure either," Aristotle said. "What I do know is that those I care about continue to live on within me."

"Everyone I cared about died a long time ago," John said. *And because I was in a coma I couldn't even say goodbye.*

"Is that so?" Aristotle eyed him. "You seem to care about your partner, this Nathan guy whom I have yet to meet."

The deep-voiced engines clicked off as the rising metal door disappeared above the entryway. John stepped through without replying to Aristotle's question. He found himself in a hexagonal room, greeted by another droning monotone announcement regarding the power status of the complex. Six massive steel panels hung overhead. Each panel curved upward to the apex of the ceiling, where they came together to form a dome. A wide, flat-screen monitor adorned each wall. All six were dark and inactive. Meanwhile, in the middle of the room, a tall gray metal chair commanded attention like an emperor's throne. In front of the chair was an expansive metal desk. It was equipped with a standard PC keyboard and a three-dimensional motion sensing pad, pieces of technology that had once been ubiquitous in every home and office.

John warily entered the room, immediately noting a pervasive foul odor. As he approached the chair, the center monitor flickered to life. Random letters and numbers materialized all across the screen. When the chaotic sequence finished, a video feed of a dark-skinned man appeared. He sported a neatly trimmed gray beard and a pair of wide, boxy rectangular glasses. A timestamp in the lower corner of the screen read October 27, 2035.

"Hello, and welcome to Mallard Island." The man's voice came from all directions, projected by the speakers along the walls.

"Howdy," Aristotle replied.

"I think it's a recording ..." John grumbled.

"Oh, sorry."

"My name is Dr. Richard Singh, Professor of Biomechanical Engineering, Emeritus, Massachusetts Institute of Technology. I was hoping to meet you, the possessor of the first and, to my knowledge, only functional spear prototype."

The professor's face grew grim. "Unfortunately, a critical failure has occurred within this facility's artificial ecosystem, leaving me with a very limited, ever-dwindling supply of food. Furthermore, I don't possess the immunity required to safely venture topside to acquire more. I have since come to terms with my fate, a fate from which I have run for many years. In any case, I'm glad that, against all odds, you've managed to discover my humble abode here on Mallard Island. I apologize for not being to greet you in person."

This guy is worse than Pierre, John thought. Why were academics always so long-winded?

The professor smiled weakly. "I imagine you have many questions about the spear grafted to your arm. For your convenience, I've compiled a document outlining its most pertinent technical specifications. I've placed said document on my desk, before you. I only request that you listen to this message in its entirety before taking it and going on your way. Please give this old soul one last chance to speak his piece."

Aristotle gave John an inquiring look. He sighed and nodded in reply. Maybe the wordy old professor would have a few nuggets of insight to share. Meanwhile, in the background the mechanical voice droned again, announcing that power was at seventy-five percent.

"You must be wondering why I decided to spend my exile from the virus here, hidden under Mallard Island." An image of the verdant island appeared beside the professor's head. "I was first charmed by Rainy Lake in the summer of 2021, when the U.S. Navy brought me here to assist in research. I was particularly drawn to Mallard Island, both for its isolated location and because I felt a certain affinity for its previous owner, Ernest Oberholtzer.

"As it happened, the island's stewards presented me with the opportunity to purchase it for a reasonable fee, so long as I promised to preserve Oberholtzer's legacy. Naturally, I jumped at the opportunity. I hope you'll agree that I have upheld my end of the bargain. My only modifications were the construction of this underground facility and the installation of solar panels on a neighboring island to collect energy — all on the U.S. Navy's dime, ostensibly for research.

"Others may have seen the purchase as an old man's vanity, but it was a carefully considered acquisition. Given the island's isolated location, I knew it would offer me at least temporary respite from the G7N3 viral outbreak that I anticipated would overrun the United States. It also seemed the perfect place to spend my twilight years in safety and peace."

"You heard of the G7N3 virus?" John whispered, glancing at Aristotle.

She shook her head. "No, but I can't imagine it'd be anything other than the Desolation virus."

"Indeed," the professor continued, "I soon realized that the island possessed a treasure trove of books, which I unfortunately haven't been able to enjoy reading since resigning myself to life in this tiny underground bunker. I hope the clues I prepared for you provided ample opportunity to explore the island and fully enjoy its amenities." A series of red lines, tracing the path from one clue to the next appeared on the image of Mallard Island. The line then reached Japanese House and the image dissolved.

"Since you're here, I assume that you heard about this island through official military channels. I made certain to record my whereabouts in the appropriate Pentagon archives. Given the risk of viral exposure, however, I made it clear that you were the only guest to whom I would grant entry into my humble abode. Death comes to us all, but I had hoped to ward it off long enough to see my creation at work.

"Likewise, I'm glad that you've survived long enough to view this video. As it happens, the battery I installed in the spear prototype had an expected lifespan of six years, and thus at the time of this recording the battery's capacity has certainly degraded severely. To compensate for this, the spear is designed to work together with the user's metabolism to supply extra energy when necessary, though even the most efficient human physiology can't generate enough raw energy to match the output of the spear's high-performance battery. Unfortunately, I wasn't able to field test the consequences of overburdening the user's metabolism." The professor rubbed the back of his neck, grimacing with embarrassment. "I can't imagine they're pleasant."

John nodded in firm agreement. The professor had confirmed what he'd suspected, that his blackouts, fatigue, and weight loss were all directly linked to his arm, the 'spear.'

"Anyhow, you're in luck," the professor continued, his expression brightening. "Using the resources available to me here, I've managed to prepare a temporary solution to this shortcoming, which you'll find along with the other documents on my desk. For a more permanent fix, I advise that you refer to the full documentation."

"Again, it's with a heavy heart that I record this video. Please forgive the impersonal delivery. As you surely know, the military is fond of secrets and thus I was never privy to your identity. I hope that you use the gift I have given you toward noble ends, and that you're able to find the power source that my colleagues were developing before it's too late."

"Dr. Richard Singh, speaking on October 27th, 2035. May you live to see the redemption of mankind."

The professor's face disappeared, and the monitor, its purpose fulfilled, clicked off.

John stared at the blank screen. The message had given him much to absorb.

"That was depressing," Aristotle said.

"Not entirely." The video had provided John with answers to the questions that had plagued him since he'd awoken from his coma over two years ago. More answers undoubtedly were provided in the documentation that Dr. Singh had prepared. John was still left to wonder, however, why Ramses, of all people, had been the one to direct him to Mallard Island.

Ramses, a youth from Frontier View who wouldn't have yet been a teenager at the time of the Desolation, had access to classified government information. This confirmed what John had previously suspected: he'd been led to Mallard Island by someone closely connected to the U.S. military.

"Let's grab the manual and get out of here," John said, approaching the throne and the desk beyond it.

As he drew near, the fetid smell of death suddenly struck him. A shudder ran down his spine. The doctor was slumped in the imposing steel chair. In his lap rested a Beretta M9. Blood had gushed from the exit wound in the crown of his head, trickling down the back of the chair and drying in a dark red pool beneath his seat. His skin was a sickly, graying black. His previously neatly trimmed beard had grown disheveled. Though the cool atmosphere in the underground complex had suppressed his rate of decomposition, it was clear that the professor had passed some time ago.

"Poor guy," Aristotle said. "He must've spent a decade down here, hoping to meet you."

"His safe haven became his tomb. I wonder how he predicted the viral outbreak."

"Well, we know that the virus, what he called the G7 ..." Aristotle trailed off.

"G7N3," John filled in.

"The G7N3 virus. We know that it was an engineered, man-made virus. It's just never been clear who unleashed it."

"But obviously he knew about it before it broke loose."

"Right, but knowing such a weapon exists and knowing it'll be set loose are two very different things."

"Hmm ..." John rubbed his beard. "Idle speculation isn't gonna help us find the answers." He looked at the desk in front of the dead man. Tucked underneath the keyboard was a packet of papers, bound together with a single large, oblong paperclip. On the cover page the Professor had written:

SPEAR
Strength and Precision Enhanced Arm Replacement

As promised, John found a bright yellow post-it note affixed to the cover. He read it to himself:

Underneath my desk is a device that will overcharge the Spear's internal battery and allow it to run at full capacity for approximately one month. Due to the high concentration of energy within, the device can be used one time and one time only. To acquire its power, hold it in your palm and clasp your fingers around it tightly (albeit not too tightly — your arm has ample strength to crush it!) for fifteen seconds. And again, please excuse me for not being able to deliver this message in person.

Best,
Dr. Richard Singh

"What's it say?" asked Aristotle.

"It says I've got a month's lease on life." John felt like a debtor who'd been given a few extra days to pay off an inordinate sum. A month would be useful only if he could find a way to permanently power his arm.

John set the stack of papers on the desk and reached underneath it. The device was attached to the desk's underside with a strong adhesive. Using his organic right arm, he yanked it free. The spherical device was the size of a baseball and constructed of an unknown metal alloy.

"Here we go," John uttered, taking the ball in his left hand and wrapping his fingers around it. It rested easily in his palm.

"Anything happening?" Aristotle asked, crossing her arms.

"The note said it would take fifteen seconds."

John tapped his boot on the steel floor. As he waited, the familiar robotic voice again crackled from the speakers.

"Power at one hundred percent of operational capacity. Life support systems, nonfunctional. Security systems, fully active."

A red light flashed throughout the room.

"Alert! Alert!" The voice announced. *"Unauthorized life form detected. Unauthorized weaponry detected. Commencing lockdown and destruction procedure, one-zero-six."*

A light breeze from the entryway blew over John's skin, rustling through the dark hairs on his forearms.

"Um ... should we get out of here?" Aristotle asked, pointing her thumb toward the exit.

"Best idea you've had all day," John said as he started for the steel door, still holding the metal ball in his hand. The wind was gaining strength, tugging at the loose fabric of his shirt.

"What about the papers on the desk?" Aristotle said, her voice struggling to cut through the howl of the wind.

John's head jerked toward the desk. The airstream was buffeting the packet of Spear documentation. The pages threatened to burst from the paper clip.

"I got it," John called out, dashing back across the room. As his hand reached for the packet, the clip broke free and the pages exploded into the air. With his left hand still clasped around the metal ball, John snatched the white sheets with his free hand, one by one. Given time, he could collect them all.

"John — the door is closing!" Aristotle shouted.

"What?"

"The door — it's going down!"

The wild breeze began to abate. Looking back, John saw the exit closing, falling slowly like a booby-trapped door in a mummy's tomb. Loose papers continued to fly about as though they'd been spit out by a copy machine gone made, creating a flurry of white chaos.

"I'll smash the door open after I get all of the papers!" John shouted.

"It's too risky! Come on!"

John growled, glancing at the few sheets of paper he'd managed to collect. To abandon the rest now would be to risk losing irreplaceable information. Yet he knew Aristotle was right.

He sprinted toward the metal door. It was already below the level of his waist and dropping fast. Holding the metal ball in one hand and the papers in the other, he leapt forward and threw his arms out above his head. His chest hit the steel floor with a heavy thud. He glided forward along the smooth surface until he'd cleared the gap — a perfect baseball slide. He half-expected to hear an umpire shout "Safe!"

"Your legs!" Aristotle yelled.

Flailing like a beached dolphin, John flung himself forward with a single desperate motion. The heavy boom of metal slamming against metal echoed through the hallway. Checking his feet, John saw that the soles of his boots had cleared the massive door by less than an inch.

It had been a close call, but he was safe — no more blustering wind, no more deafening alarm, no more annoying robotic voice. All that remained was the dead quiet of the abandoned underground facility. John relaxed his arms, resting them on the cold metal floor.

An explosion roared from behind the closed door, like a bunker buster going off in a bank vault. The complex shook with the violence of an earthquake and a heavy object crashed into the steel door, leaving a dent worthy of a pair of iron giants with a titanium battering ram.

"I don't think you would've survived that one," Aristotle said, her eyes wide with shock. "He certainly made sure no unauthorized persons would see his work."

John grunted as he let his head drop, lying supine on the floor. Meanwhile the ball in his left hand began to glow, pulsating in harmony with a shotgun shell-sized rectangular patch located on his upper arm. A surge of energy ran through the limb like a bolt of lightning, and with it a renewed sense of vitality coursed through his veins.

He drew his knees to his chest and then thrust his legs forward, jumping to his feet. Though his muscles were still weak, it felt like he'd cast off a suit of chain mail that had weighed down his every move. Strength and agility long forgotten rushed back into his body.

The ball in his hand had done its job. John now had a month to find a permanent solution or suffer the consequences, the extent of which he still didn't fully understand. He released his grip on the spherical charger, now spent. It hit the metal with a deep, resounding clang. John turned his attention to the slim fistful papers in his other hand.

"Come on," Aristotle urged. "Let's get out of here before the doomsday device finds another way to liquidate us. The papers can wait 'til we get topside. We still gotta find our missing persons."

Nathan! In the frenetic commotion John had forgotten about his partner. He obviously wasn't down here, but then where was he? Surely on the island somewhere.

"Let's head up." John gestured toward the small elevator at the end of the hallway. "I found what I came to the island for. Now it's time to track down the people we lost along the way."

Chapter 26

LIFTING ARISTOTLE and John back up to fresh air, the elevator platform jerked to a sudden halt. Everything in Japanese house was just as it had been. The ornate Chinese characters still decorated the floor and outside the early afternoon sun still shone brightly.

Aristotle followed John off the elevator. The platform's motor returned to life and it descended into the darkness below. The wooden floorboards slid back into place, covering the entrance. The only evidence of the explosion below was a screen window that had dislodged from its frame and was now precariously leaning inward, threating to crash onto the floor. Like a time capsule, the professor's complex would remain underneath the island, a forlorn reminder of a bygone era.

"Think we were the first ones to learn of the existence of the professor's chamber?" Aristotle asked.

"No." John shook his head. "Someone told us to come here. They must've known what we'd find down there. But I'd guess they also knew about the trap and didn't want to risk triggering it themselves, which means we probably were the first to venture down there."

"Who told you about the island?"

"A kid named Ramses."

"What's he look like?

"About my height. Athletic build. Short blonde hair, sharp blue eyes, and an arrogant, know-it-all attitude."

"I think I've met him, too," Aristotle said. John had described all of the young man's most notable features exactly.

"Your boyfriend?" John said, dryly.

Aristotle rolled her eyes. "If we're talking about the same guy, then he's the one who told me you were coming here. One of the General's men."

"I see. After we find our missing partners, I'd like to hear more about this 'General.'"

"I'll gladly tell you what I know," Aristotle said.

"All in due time." John shoved open the door that led to the screened-in porch around Japanese house and exited. Aristotle trailed a step behind.

"Well, look who we have here." The gruff voice barked from just beside the doorframe. "If it ain't the legendary John Osborne and his Greek philosopher sidekick."

"Gallagher?" Aristotle said. "We thought you'd been kidnapped or —" She cut herself short when she noticed the pump action shotgun in Gallagher's hands, trained on her and John.

"Hands up, both of you," Gallagher ordered.

"You know this guy?" John asked, raising his hands in a show of surrender.

"I thought I did," Aristotle said, lifting her arms sky high. "What the Desolation is this about, Gallagher?"

"Business, sister, business." Gallagher spit, the dark wad of saliva splattering on the wood floor. "You folks ain't the only ones with skin in the game here. Now tell me — where is it?"

"What?" Aristotle blinked, confused. A shotgun in her face couldn't make her answer a question she didn't understand.

"You know," Gallagher growled. "The Northland Core."

Neither Aristotle nor John responded. If John knew what Gallagher was talking about, he wasn't betraying his knowledge.

"You really know how to choose your men," John grumbled.

"Not now, John," Aristotle growled. How could he crack jokes at a time like this? Panic rising, her throat tightened as the shotgun remained trained on her.

"Hey — no lover talk! Now where in God's name is the Northland Core?" Gallagher itched at the trigger of his shotgun. "Either you give me the info or you give me your lives. What's it gonna be?"

"I'm getting more of a 'you give me the info *and* you give me your lives' vibe," Aristotle said.

"Same here," John agreed.

"Well, now ain't you got me all figured out?" Gallagher eyed his captives warily. "Tell you the truth, I think the General would prefer you alive — especially you, Osborne — but my orders don't specify either way. This is my show."

He's one of the General's men. Of course, Aristotle thought. The General's boot print was stamped all over the North, his influence ever expanding. Now he'd trapped her and John like a pair of beavers at the edge of a waterfall. She knew John was a fast draw, but even he wouldn't dare test a trained soldier armed with a locked and loaded shotgun from three yards out.

"Look, I don't know about this Northland Core. I can give you these documents in my hand," John said. "They're all we could salvage from down there."

"What do they say?" Gallagher asked.

"We didn't get a chance to read them." John said, making a throat-clearing noise.

"Seems like you've lost your touch, Osborne."

John frowned. "You know me?"

"By reputation. You think you're the only ex-Marine who survived the Desolation?" Gallagher snickered. "I bet that scraggly rat's nest of a beard has got your commanding officer turning in his grave."

"You'll be able to ask him soon enough."

"I reckon it'll be you doing the askin', Osborne."

"We'll see," John replied with a calm confidence. "Here's what I suggest: I set the documents on the ground over there." He nodded toward the grass behind Gallagher. "You take them and leave on the sailboat. We wait here until you're long gone, and then we look for our own way off this rock. Deal?"

Gallagher's lips curved into a sinister smile. "Or I could just shoot you and take the papers."

"And risk damaging them? Besides, you wouldn't want to trigger my arm's terminal defense system."

"Terminal defense system?" Gallagher frowned. "What the hell is that?"

"You don't wanna find out."

Gallagher snorted. "Fine. We'll do things your way. Step toward the grass, slowly." He glanced at Aristotle. "Don't try anything funny, sister."

"I'm going to move forward now," John said, cautiously taking a step.

Gallagher nodded. He backpedaled toward the grass, keeping his shotgun trained on John.

"Osborne, you're giving him our only bargaining chip ..." Aristotle warned.

"It's okay. What was lost is found."

What was lost is found? What is he talking about? Careful not to be conspicuous, Aristotle gazed past Gallagher, down the rocky path that led back toward the center of the island. If Osborne had found something, it could only be out there. To her surprise she spotted movement — an animal creeping amid the thick green underbrush, perhaps?

John and Gallagher stared at each other as they stepped off the Japanese House porch and into the surrounding grassy area.

"I'm going to set the papers down and back away," John said, his back facing Aristotle.

"Go ahead," Gallagher replied with a smug grin.

John set the papers on the ground. Gallagher, keeping his shotgun steady against his shoulder, slowly knelt and snatched the documents from the ground. He shoved them in his back pocket as he stood back up, then returned his free hand to the barrel of his shotgun.

"A terminal defense system?" Gallagher said, mockingly. "That the best you can come up with?"

"For your sake, I hope you don't try to find out," John replied, flatly.

"John Osborne. Full of shit to his last breath."

"This is your last chance to walk away."

Gallagher snickered. "Keep hell warm for me." He took aim at John's upper chest, preparing to send a volley of buckshot into the bearded man.

Aristotle felt her chest tighten. She had to reach for her gun and shoot Gallagher before he shot John.

She had to try.

A gunshot rang out. Aristotle's hand instinctively reached for her holster.

Desolation! Too late!

She expected John to collapse in a heap. Instead, Gallagher flew towards John, careening forward like a marionette that'd had its strings jerked. John stood tall as Gallagher's body crashed to the ground.

"What the Desolation?" Aristotle uttered, eyes wide. She moved toward John and Gallagher. In the back of Gallagher's skull, she saw a large bore entrance wound — the mark of a high-caliber rifle round or a shotgun slug.

In the distance, a young man with dark hair and tan skin rose from behind the cover of bushes. He triumphantly lifted a long-barreled gun above his head.

"Our other missing person reappeared just in time," John said. Stepping past Gallagher's corpse, he jogged toward the man, Nathan. Aristotle trotted behind.

Nathan took a deep breath and sat down on the grass. He crossed his legs and set the shotgun, a Remington 870, on his lap.

John knelt beside Nathan. "That's a nasty bruise," he said, remarking about the ugly blackish-purple splotch that stretched across the left side of Nathan's forehead. "What happened?"

"That guy," Nathan said, nodding toward where Gallagher had stood, "he knocked me out. When I woke up, I was in front house. My arm and legs were bound with tape."

Aristotle took a knee. "Do you have a concussion?"

Nathan shook his head. "No, I think I'm okay." He looked toward John. "Who is she?"

"I haven't quite figured that out myself," John replied. "She calls herself Aristotle."

Nathan grinned. "Aristotle. Not what I would've guessed, but I like it." Though he looked exhausted, he appeared to be in good spirits.

"Nathan," John said, "had you ever killed a man before?"

Nathan shook his head. "No."

"Are you holding up alright?"

Nathan paused, sighing and looking toward the ground.

"You know," he said, "I was at home with my mom when she died, years ago. I saw some of my friends die around that time, too. I saw corpses, scattered about the streets of Minneapolis. And last year I was at my dad's side when he passed away." He raised his head, looking John in the eye. "Today is the first time I saw death help a friend instead of take one away. I think I can live with a little blood on my hands."

"How'd you know what Gallagher was up to?" Aristotle asked.

"Well, I woke up in the Wannigan, and I heard him outside, shouting into a radio. It sounded like he was coming after you. By then, I'd already guessed that the final clue was pointing us to Japanese House, so I put two and two together and came this way.

"When I arrived, the man was already staked out in front, so I sat tight and watched from afar. You two appeared a bit later. The conversation between the three of you didn't sound so friendly, so I crept closer to look for a clean shot, just in case it came to that.

"For a moment, I thought the man would leave peacefully and I wouldn't have to pull the trigger. When he made his intention clear, though, I didn't think twice before doing what had to be done." Nathan looked John in the eye. "Thanks for giving me a good angle."

"It's me who should be thanking you, kid," John said. "One more question. You said you were tied up. How'd you free yourself?"

"Remember that bottle of wine you brought back from the Wannigan a few nights ago? I wiggled over to it, kicked it until it shattered against the wall, and used a piece of glass to cut my wrists and legs free."

"You're acquiring the taste, I see," John said.

Nathan frowned, leaving Aristotle uncertain as to what dissonant chord John had struck with his dry wit.

"Enough about me," Nathan said. "How about you? Seems you suddenly have a lot of pep."

"Never felt better," John said. "After we tidy up around here, we can head back to the Wannigan and I'll tell you all about it."

"What about our friend over there?" Aristotle tilted her head toward Gallagher's corpse. "Are we just going to leave his body to the wolves?"

John gave a grunt, making his contempt clear. Despite that, he reluctantly made his way back toward Japanese House and Gallagher's body, leading the way for Aristotle and Nathan. After some discussion, the three of them decided that the professor's underground complex would make a suitable tomb. They took Gallagher's shotgun and radio, then called up the elevator platform, placed his still-clothed corpse on it, and let it descend back into the darkness.

Gallagher was fortunate. His unceremonious burial was more than most victims of the Desolation had received.

Chapter 27

A FEW HOURS LATER Nathan, John, and Aristotle sat together at the dining table in the Wannigan. The evening sun made its presence known, painting the hardwood walls of houseboat soft yellow with its dying light.

Nathan listened as John and Aristotle chatted, first about the General and then about John's arm. According to Aristotle, the General was a man who wanted to shift the balance of power in the north, claiming the majority for himself, naturally. Based on Aristotle's information, it seemed likely that the General had had a hand in Emiko's kidnapping. Just thinking about it made Nathan's blood boil.

Next, John told Aristotle about his arm. This was old news to Nathan, and soon he tuned out, instead turning his attention to the meager documentation that John had salvaged from the underground chamber. His head, still hurting from Gallagher's blow, throbbed as he paged through it.

Only four and a half pages of the documentation had survived. The tempest that had raged through the professor's quarters had left the sheets in tatters. Making matters worse, the professor had written the notes on unlined paper in compact, difficult-to-decipher cursive letters. As Nathan studied the documentation, he reminded himself that they had just one month to find a permanent solution to John's energy sapping arm.

Unfortunately, Nathan found that the pages which John had rescued from incineration contained more technical details than practical information. He had hoped to discover the full extent of the Spear's capabilities and the source of its power, not a dry description of the inner workings of its pneumatic systems.

John and Aristotle fell silent. John rose from the table.

"What do you make of those notes, riddle-master?" he asked as he paced back and forth.

"They're dense. Cryptic. Completely usele ..." Nathan trailed off, running his finger across a line of text at the bottom of a page. "Maybe not. Here we go. The professor writes, 'As of 2027, the Spear's intended power source, a device known as the Northland Core, was being developed in Minneapolis, Minnesota. The project was a cooperative effort between the ...'" Nathan's eyes reached the bottom of the page. He flipped it over to check the other side.

"Cooperative effort between the ...?" John prompted.

"I don't know." Nathan shuffled through the pages. "That's the end of the page and don't I have the next one."

"Hammersnap," John cursed, pounding his fist against his thigh in frustration. "Is this the only lead we have to go on? Tracking down this Northland Core could be harder than finding a deer tick in the fur of a frankenmoose."

"Frankenmoose?" Aristotle furrowed her brow, confused and amused.

"John has an irrational hatred of tvapas," Nathan said. "And resorts to calling them names."

Aristotle held back a snicker. "That so? We don't see many of them near Toronto, actually, but just the same, they seem harmless enough. Anyhow, you know the Northland Core is in Minneapolis, right?"

"I suppose," Nathan said. He knew Minneapolis. He'd grown up there. Once a burgeoning metropolis, the city was now a vast, sprawling wasteland of decay and dilapidation — or so he'd heard. Without any further information it would be nearly impossible to find the Core. Still, he saw little choice but to try.

"Let's consider the facts," John said.

"What you need is in Minneapolis. What else is there to consider?" Nathan asked.

"Motive."

"Motive?"

"Think about it." John extended a finger. "Who directed us here?"

"Ramses," Nathan replied, setting the professor's notes on the table.

"Who is likely working for the General," Aristotle added.

"Right," John said. "And why would the General want us to come here?"

"Because your arm was the key to safely entering the professor's complex," Aristotle suggested. "Our little run-in with security made that pretty clear, I'd say."

John glared at Aristotle. "A mishap that wouldn't have happened if you hadn't followed us here."

"You wouldn't have even found the professor's chamber without —"

"In any case," John cut Aristotle off, "we're only pawns in this game. The General had a deeper motive for sending us here."

"And what is his motive, then?" Aristotle retorted.

"Easy: he wants power," Nathan offered. "The Northland Core is obviously a power source, one with enough energy to keep your arm functioning indefinitely. That's why we need to find it. It's only natural, then, that a man after power, a man like the General, would want to get his hands on it, too."

"Bingo." John pointed at Nathan. "The General wants this Northland Core, but he doesn't know where it is. He believed that the professor knew its location, so he lured us here to obtain that information. Once we secured the documents from the professor's complex, we became expendable."

"Are you so sure? Killing us didn't seem to be part of the agenda," Aristotle said. "From what I could tell, Gallagher was only going to kill us to ensure his escape."

"Either way, it was nice of him to spare us," John said. "Too bad nice guys finish last."

No one spoke for a time after that. Outside the Wannigan, the haunting, tremolo cry of a loon carried across the lake, echoing through the stillness of the evening.

"So, what's the plan?" Nathan said.

"We go to Minneapolis," John said.

"All of us?" Nathan asked.

"Not all of us," Aristotle said. "Now that I got things sorted out with you, Osborne, I have other obligations."

"The General?" John said.

"Right. I'd ask you to help me look for him, but I understand that you have more pressing concerns."

Nathan's stomach growled loudly, interrupting the conversation. "Aristotle, did you bring any food with you on that sailboat? It's been a while since I've had anything to eat."

"For you? Sure thing," Aristotle nodded and disappeared outside, the door of the Wannigan gently knocking against the door frame behind her.

John took a seat at the long, wooden dining table. "You mind that we're not going back to Frontier View just yet?" he asked. "You know you can return on your own, if you want."

"Go home now? You can't get rid of me that easily, John," Nathan said. "The adventure is just beginning."

"Glad to hear it, kid."

I'm just glad I'm finally making myself useful, Nathan thought, tapping his fingers on the table as he waited for dinner. He imagined it would taste better than any meal he'd ever had before.

* * *

Aristotle traversed the pier toward Gallagher's sailboat. The waning sunlight reflected from the glassy surface of Rainy Lake.

Had Gallagher even been the man's real name? The initials on his cigarette lighter suggested it was, but it could've been just another sticky strand in the web of lies he'd weaved.

She stepped onto the boat, noting that her backpack was still in the tiny storage compartment. *This boat probably wasn't really his, either*, she thought with disgust. Finding an abandoned boat to ferry her to the island wouldn't have been any trouble. Thanks to the Desolation, there were likely more boats left in the world than people.

As she gathered an armful of rations for Nathan and John, she considered her next move. She'd promised to keep in touch with Captain Griswold. It had been weeks since she'd contacted him. She owed him a call. Would Gallagher's radio allow her to access his office in Toronto? She'd find out soon enough.

Lost in thought, she surveyed the serene lake. Would her family have been proud of what she'd become, a vagabond in search of her own breed of justice? The gentle slap of waves on the rocky shore offered no answers. Aristotle took the food she'd gathered and headed back to the Wannigan. Maybe one day, soon, the promise of the future would be bright enough to drive out the shadows of the past.

Later that night, a stiff breeze sprang up, gently rattling the Wannigan's windows. During dinner, there was a brief debate as to what to do with Gallagher's possessions. Ultimately, they agreed that John would inherit Gallagher's shotgun and Aristotle his radio. Feeling contented and exhausted, each of the three found a bed on the island and went to sleep. At dawn the next morning, with the wind at their backs, they set sail for the mainland, returning to the dock from which Aristotle had departed.

"Which way are you boys going?" Aristotle asked after they'd come ashore.

"South. We gotta retrieve our frankenmoose from a friend. Then we'll continue on to Minneapolis," John said, pointing toward International Falls.

"Then this is where we part ways. I'm probably heading back north, at least for the time being. It's been … " Aristotle paused, searching for the correct word. "It's been an invigorating experience." Next, she approached Nathan and leaned in to give him a kiss on the cheek. "Thanks for saving us back there. I owe you one."

Nathan blushed. He opened his mouth to speak, but no words came out.

She turned to John. "As for you, Osborne, I hope we find ourselves on the same side again in the future."

"Likewise," John replied, offering a tired smile.

With that, Aristotle turned her back to the two men and quickened her pace along the frontage road that led back to the weather-worn blacktop of the Trans-Canada Highway. She was alone once again.

She pulled the radio out of her pack and tuned it to the Toronto police department's frequency. Given the distance, she was unsure if it would work, and even if the signal reached Toronto, she didn't know if the department would have anyone monitoring radio transmissions. Still, she had to try.

Where to next? Hopefully Captain Griswold would have an answer. Aristotle stared at the radio apprehensively, then hit send.

Chapter 28

RAMSES SAT RIGHT where he always had, stoically enduring the stale air of the Restoration Army's comm room. He passed the hours under the room's harsh white lights by alternatively staring at the wall and reading *The Call of the Wild*. Late in the afternoon a voice erupted from the radio, catching him off guard.

"Private — you copy?" It was the General.

"Yes, sir."

"A question for you: Has Lieutenant Bogues' reported any activity in the past few hours?"

Ramses consulted his notes.

"There was a transmission from the lieutenant's radio at one six three seven, sir. However, it appears he was using a non-official frequency, sir."

"Just as I suspected. Private, your time in communications may soon be ending."

"Sir?" Ramses inquired. It was as close as he could come to asking "why" without breaching protocol.

"Lieutenant Gallagher Bogues is MIA — likely dead. I believe Osborne and company are making their way here. I'd like you to be a part of the welcoming committee."

"So he found what you wanted him to find on Mallard Island, sir?"

"I believe so. And next he's going to unwittingly lead us to what we've been tearing up this city trying to unearth."

"The Northland Core, sir?"

"Yes. Report to me first thing tomorrow morning at zero seven hundred hours. I need your assistance in making the necessary preparations."

"Roger that, sir."

"Excellent. The General, over and out."

The radio clicked off. Ramses closed his book and slid it to a far corner of the table. He had to ready himself. A second meeting with John Osborne was an opportunity he intended to be prepared for.

Chapter 29

JANICE SAT BEHIND the counter in the Lakefront Inn's office, waiting for potential guests. Today she and Emiko were the only staff on hand. While Janice manned the desk, Emiko hurried around the premises, cleaning up the rooms as guests checked out.

Emiko was a hard worker, Janice had to admit. Though she'd been apprehensive about bringing the teenage girl on board, her decision to do so had been a good one. Previously, she'd had to both clean the rooms and handle reception duties. Now she had time to undertake maintenance tasks that had long been neglected. This morning she had repainted the Vacancy and No Vacancy signs, and was presently straightening up the office desk.

Staring at the poster on the wall, of a pristine Hawaiian beach, she wondered if she'd ever get a chance to visit Hawaii, or any kind of tropical seaside paradise. Even getting to the coast, to California or Mexico, was practically unthinkable now. Too far, too dangerous, and even if she arrived at the coast, she didn't know what she'd find. Even before the Desolation had wiped out mankind, civil war across the U.S. had taken its toll. For all she knew, Los Angeles was a nuclear wasteland.

The door chime jangled as two men, Smitty and Leonard, entered. Somehow the unusual duo had procured a working vehicle, an old black Honda. She didn't know where they'd gotten it, nor did she care. Between the scarcity of gasoline and the notoriety that would come with driving a motorized vehicle around, owning a car would be more trouble that it was worth.

"Why, hello there. What can I do for you this fine day?" she asked, smiling courteously.

"We'll be checking out today, ma'am," Smitty, the burlier of the two men, said. "It's been a pleasant stay, but we need to move along."

"It's been our pleasure to have you, gentlemen," Janice said. "I don't suppose you could leave that car behind for me, could you?"

Smitty grinned, showing his teeth. "I'm afraid not, ma'am. But who knows? Maybe someday soon, you'll be able to buy a car of your own."

"Is that so?" Janice said, feigning intrigue. In truth, she didn't put much stock in what these two men had to say. A little friendly chit-chat, however, could only bolster the hotel's reputation and bottom line.

"Times are changing. The world is getting back to how it was. Just you wait." Smitty gave her a flirtatious wink.

Janice merely smiled in reply. Beyond the front window, she caught a glimpse of Emiko, standing beside the black Honda in the parking lot. *What is that girl up to?*

"Just you wait is right," Leonard added. "Next time we come back this way, we'll be bringin' good news."

"I do like what I'm hearing, though it sounds a bit mysterious to me," Janice said, acting coy. Outside, Emiko had popped open the trunk of the black sedan and was rummaging through it. She had a backpack and a fearsome-looking rifle strapped across her back.

Janice bit her lip. She didn't know what Emiko was up to, but she trusted Emiko more than she trusted these two goons. She decided she'd prolong the conversation to buy Emiko a bit more time. She could give the girl that much — followed by a scolding later, if necessary.

"Mind if I ask where you're off to?" she asked.

Leonard jumped at the chance to reply. "We're heading back to —"

Smitty shot him a hard glare, stopping him short. "I'm afraid that's confidential, ma'am. For the time being, at least. Maybe next time we'll be able to tell you a bit more about ourselves, over coffee or beer. The Drunken Loon has quite a fine selection on tap."

"Stop by next time you're in town and I'll consider it. Have to say, though, that you won't find much coffee around here, save for the imitation chicory root variety."

"We may be able to find you some coffee and bring it up this way," Leonard said. "Have ourselves a good old-fashioned coffee hour."

Janice smiled. "You know where to find me."

Outside, Emiko crawled into the black car's trunk and closed the lid. Did she know that trunks couldn't be opened from the inside?

"Anyhow, we'd best be going," Smitty said, turning for the door. "We'll look forward to having that cup of coffee with you."

"Thanks for the room, ma'am," Leonard added.

"The pleasure was all ours. Have a safe trip to wherever the roads may lead you next."

"Will do," Smitty said, giving her a smile and a nod before leading Leonard out. The door chime clanked again. Janice watched nervously as the two men got in their car, Smitty taking the wheel. The car crossed the parking lot and soon disappeared around the corner, taking Emiko with it.

What is that girl thinking? Janice wondered. She'd been coming to like Emiko and would miss the tenacious girl's companionship. She shook her head and exhaled deeply. She didn't expect Emiko would be returning. Hopefully, the girl knew what she was doing — and had a way to get out of that trunk.

Suddenly left without her helping hand, she morosely put out her "Be Back Shortly" sign and left the office to tidy up the vacant hotel rooms on her own. The two men, whatever their real intentions, had been right about one thing: The times were a-changin'.

About The Author

Henry J. Olsen grew up as a quiet kid in a small Wisconsin town. Now he travels the world and writes tales of adventure.

As of this writing he eats, sleeps, and writes in Kaohsiung, Taiwan.

Follow him via his blog:
http://simplyunbound.com

Also by Henry J. Olsen

The Northland Chronicles
Spear Hunter
Desolation's Wake (Coming in 2015)

Northland Adventures
Ramses Thunder

Other Works
Bullies

See you in the Minneapple.

www.ingramcontent.com/pod-product-compliance
Lightning Source LLC
Chambersburg PA
CBHW071237130626
46556CB00003B/1044